PENGUIN BOOKS

# SPRING

Karl Ove Knausgaard's first novel, *Out of the World*, was the first ever debut novel to win the Norwegian Critics' Prize and his second, *A Time for Everything*, was widely acclaimed. The *My Struggle* cycle of novels has been heralded as a masterpiece wherever it has appeared, and the first volume was awarded the prestigious Brage Prize.

\* \* \*

## Praise for *Spring*

"Poignant and beautiful . . . Even if you think you won't like Knausgaard, try this one and you'll get him and get why some of us have gone crazy for him."                                          —*Los Angeles Review of Books*

"Knausgaard has assembled this living encyclopedia for his daughter with a wild and desperate sort of love, as a way to forge her attachment to the world, to fasten her to it—to fight the family legacy of becoming unmoored and alienated. Fall in love with the world, he enjoins, stay sensitive to it, stay in it."                    —*The New York Times*

"Knausgaard's assets are on full display, including his precise writing style and his unerring sense of detail. He is constantly attuned to his surroundings, noting the changing weather and the colors of flowers, which may account for why he is so successful at what he does: transforming quotidian life into drama. . . . For anyone who is curious about this writer but has not felt the urge to invest in the full 3,500 pages of his autobiographical series, *My Struggle*, *Spring* makes for an excellent introduction. It is the shortest book he has ever written, but it is all muscle, a generous slice of a thoughtful, ruminative life."                        —*The Washington Post*

"A fine stand-alone meditation on mortality and fatherhood."
                                               —*Kirkus Reviews* (starred review)

"This is a remarkably honest take on the strange linkages between love, loss, laughter, and self-destruction, a perfect distillation of Knausgaard's unique gifts."                    —*Publishers Weekly* (starred review)

D0289016

# SPRING
# KARL OVE KNAUSGAARD

With illustrations by Anna Bjerger

Translated from the Norwegian by Ingvild Burkey

Penguin Books

PENGUIN BOOKS
An imprint of Penguin Random House LLC
penguinrandomhouse.com

Originally published in Norwegian under the title *Om våren*
by Forlaget Oktober, Oslo, 2016
English-language edition first published in Great Britain by Harvill Secker,
an imprint of Penguin Random House UK, 2018
First published in the United States of America by Penguin Press,
an imprint of Penguin Random House LLC, 2018
Published in Penguin Books 2019

Illustrations by Anna Bjerger

Excerpt from *Private Confessions* by Ingmar Bergman, translated by Joan Tate
(Arcade Publishing, 1997).
Excerpt from "London Calling" written by Joe Strummer and Mick Jones.

ISBN 9780399563386 (paperback)

THE LIBRARY OF CONGRESS HAS CATALOGED THE HARDCOVER EDITION AS FOLLOWS:
Names: Knausgard, Karl Ove, 1968– author. | Bjerger, Anna illustrator. |
   Burkey, Ingvild, 1967– translator.
Title: Spring / Karl Ove Knausgaard ; with illustrations by Anna Bjerger ;
   translated from the Norwegian by Ingvild Burkey.
Other titles: Om vêaren. English
Description: New York, : Penguin Press, 2018. |
Identifiers: LCCN 2018006367 (print) | LCCN 2018011738 (ebook) |
   ISBN 9780399563379 (ebook) | ISBN 9780399563362 (hardcover)
Subjects: | BISAC: Fiction / Biographical. | Biography & Autobiography /
   Personal Memoirs. | Biography & Autobiography / Literary.
Classification: LCC PT8951.21.N38 (ebook) | LCC PT8951.21.N38 O5513 2018
   (print) | DDC 839.823/74—dc23
LC record available at https://lccn.loc.gov/2018006367

Printed in the United States of America
10  9  8  7  6  5  4  3  2  1

Set in Scala

# Spring

ONE

You don't know what air is, yet you breathe. You don't know what sleep is, yet you sleep. You don't know what night is, yet you lie in it. You don't know what a heart is, yet your own heart beats steadily in your chest, day and night, day and night, day and night.

You are three months old and as if swaddled in routines you lie on a bed of sameness through the days, for you don't have a cocoon like larvae do, you don't have a pouch like the kangaroos, you don't have a den like the badgers or the bears. You have your bottle of milk, you have the changing table with nappies and wet wipes, you have the pram with the pillow and the duvet, you have your parents' large warm bodies. Surrounded by all this you grow so slowly that no one notices, least of all yourself, for first you grow outwards, by gripping and holding on to the things around you with your hands, your mouth, your eyes, your thoughts, thereby bringing them into being, and only when you have done this for a few years and the world has been constituted do you begin to discover all that grips you, and you grow inwardly too, towards yourself.

What is the world like to a newborn baby?

Light, dark. Cold, warm. Soft, hard.

The whole array of objects in a house, all meaning

deriving from the relations within a family, the significance that every person dwells within, all this is invisible, hidden not by the darkness but by the light of the undifferentiated.

Someone once told me that heroin is so fantastic because the feelings it awakens are akin to those we have as children, when everything is taken care of, the feeling of total security we bask in then, which is so fundamentally good. Anyone who has experienced that high wants to experience it again, since they know it exists as a possibility.

The life I live is separated from yours by an abyss. It is full of problems, of conflicts, of duties, of things that have to be taken care of, handled, fixed, of wills that must be satisfied, wills that must be resisted and perhaps wounded, all in a continual stream where almost nothing stands still but everything is in motion and everything has to be parried.

I am forty-six years old and that is my insight, that life is made up of events that have to be parried. And that the moments of happiness in life all have to do with the opposite. ·

What is the opposite of parrying something?

It isn't to regress, it isn't to withdraw into your world of light and dark, warm and cold, soft and hard. Nor is it the light of the undifferentiated, it is neither sleep nor rest. The opposite of parrying is creating, making, adding something that wasn't there before.

You were not there before.


Love is not a word I often use, it seems too big in relation to the life I live, the world I know. But then I grew up in a culture that was careful with words. My mother has never told me she loves me, and I have never told her I love her. The same goes for my brother. If I were to say to my mother or my brother that I love them, they would be horrified. I would have laid a burden on them, violently upsetting the balance between us, almost as if I had staggered around in a drunken fit during a child's christening.

When you were born I knew nothing about you, yet I was filled with feelings for you, overwhelming at first, for a birth is overwhelming, even to someone who is merely looking on – it is as if everything in the room grows denser, as if a kind of gravity develops that draws all meaning towards it, so that for a few hours it can only be found there, later becoming more evenly spread out, subjected to the everyday, diluted with the eventlessness of all the hours of the day and yet always there.

I am your father, and you know my face, my voice and my ways of holding you, but beyond that I could be anyone to you, filled with anything. My own father, your grandfather, who is dead, spent his last years with his mother, and their existence was pitiless. He was an alcoholic and had regressed, he no longer had the strength to parry anything, he had let everything slide, just sat there drinking. That he did so in his mother's home is significant. She had given birth to him, she had cared for him and carried him here and there, made sure he was warm, dry, fed. The bond this created between them was never broken. He tried, I know that, but he couldn't do it. That's why he stayed there. There he could let himself go to ruin. No matter how crippled, no matter how hideous, it was also love. Somewhere deep within there was love, unconditional love.

Back then I didn't have children, so I didn't understand it. I saw only the hideousness, the unfreedom, the regression. Now I know. Love is many things, most of its forms are fleeting, linked to everything that happens, everything that comes and goes, everything that fills us at first, then empties us out, but unconditional love is constant, it glows faintly throughout one's whole life, and I want you to know this – that you too were born into that love, and that it will envelop you, no matter what happens, as long as your mother and I are alive.

It may happen that you don't want anything to do with it. It may happen that you turn away from it. And one day you will understand that it doesn't matter, that it doesn't change anything, that unconditional love is the only love that doesn't bind you but sets you free.

The love that binds one is something else, it is another form of love, less pure, more mixed up with the person who loves, and it has greater force, it can overshadow everything else, even destroy. Then it must be parried.

I don't know what your life will be like, I don't know what will happen to us, but I know what your life is like now, and how we are doing now, and since you won't remember any of it, not the least little thing, I will tell you about one day in our life, the first spring you were with us. You had thin hair, it looked reddish in the light, and it grew unevenly; there was a circle on the back of your head with no hair at all, probably because it was nearly always pressing against something, pillows and rugs, sofas and chairs, but I still found it strange, for surely your hair wasn't like grass, which grows only where the sun shines and air is flowing?

Your face was round, your mouth was small, but your lips were relatively wide, and your eyes were round and rather large. You slept in a cot at one end of the house, with a mobile of African animals dangling above you, while I slept in a bed next to yours, for it was my job to look after you at night, since your mother was sensitive when it came to sleep, whereas I slept heavily, like a child, no matter what happened around me. Sometimes you would wake at night and scream because you were hungry, but since I didn't wake up or only heard it as a sound coming from far, far away, you learned the hard way not to expect anything while it was dark, so that after only a few weeks you slept through the night, from when you were put to bed at six in the evening until you woke up at six in the morning.

This morning began like all the others. You woke up in the darkness and started to scream.

What time was it?

I fumbled around for my phone, which should be on the windowsill just above my head.

There it was.

The light from the screen, no larger than my hand, filled nearly the entire dark room with a vague glow.

Twenty to six.

'Oh, it's still early, little girl,' I said and sat up. The movement set off a rustling, wheezing sound in my chest, and I coughed for a while.

You had gone quiet.

I walked the two steps over to the cot and bent over you, placed a hand on either side of your little ribcage and lifted you up, holding you close to my chest and supporting the back of your head and neck with one hand, even though you were already able to hold your head up by yourself.

'Hi there,' I said. 'Did you sleep well?'

You breathed calmly and seemed to press your cheek against my chest.

I carried you down the hall and into the bathroom. Through the window I saw a narrow band of light just above the eastern horizon, reddish against the black sky and the black ground. The house was cold, the night had been starlit and the temperature must have dropped, but fortunately the dryer had been on all night, and some of its heat, which at times seems almost tropical, still lingered in the room.

I laid you down carefully on the changing table, which had been squeezed in between the bath and the sink, coughing again. A glob of mucus came loose in my throat, I spat it into the sink, turned on the tap to wash it down, saw how it clung to the metal wall of the plughole, smooth and sticky, while water ran over it on both sides until it slowly began to slide over to one side and then, abruptly as if acting of its own volition, disappeared down the drain. I glanced briefly at the mirror above the sink, saw my own masklike face staring at me, turned off the tap and bent over you.

You looked up at me. If you were thinking about something, it couldn't have been put into words or concepts, it couldn't be anything you formulated to yourself, only something you felt. *There he is*, is maybe what you felt as you looked at me, and along with the face you recognised came a whole set of other feelings associated with what I usually did with you and in what ways. A great deal must still have been vague and open within you, like the shifting light in the sky, but once in a while everything must have fused together and become definite and unavoidable: those were the basic bodily sensations, the tide of hunger, the tide of thirst, the tide of tiredness, the tide of too hot and too cold. Those were the times you started to cry.

'What are you thinking?' I said to distract you a little as I undid the top buttons of your white pyjamas. But you still thrust out your lower lip, and your mouth began to quiver. With my index finger I struck the tail of one of the little wooden aeroplanes hanging above the changing table so that it began revolving. Then I did the same with the next one, and the next after that.

'Don't tell me you're going to fall for that same old trick today too?' I said.

But you did. You stared wide-eyed at all the movement in the air while I took off your pyjamas. As I put them in the laundry basket, steps sounded on the ceiling above us. It must have been your younger sister, since the elder one always slept as long as she could and your brother was probably up already. I loosened the flaps of the nappy and pulled it off. As I carried it over to the waste bin it felt unexpectedly heavy, as nappies often do, since the material creates an expectation of lightness. That weight felt good, it told me that you were all right, that your body was functioning as it should. Everything else seemed to be falling apart, from the fluorescent tube above the stove, which had begun blinking more than a year ago and then gone out completely, and which still remained uselessly in its socket, to the car, which had suddenly begun to vibrate whenever it passed a certain speed and had been collected by a tow truck and taken to a garage – to say nothing of all the food that got mouldy or spoilt, shirt buttons that fell off or zips that got stuck, the dishwasher which had stopped functioning or the kitchen sink drainpipe which had got clogged somewhere in the garden, probably with congealed grease, the plumber said when he came to fix it. But the bodies of the children in our house, so smooth and soft on the outside, and infinitely more complex than any machine or mechanical device on the inside, had always functioned perfectly, had never broken down, had never gone to pieces.

I put on a new nappy, widened the opening of a romper suit with my hands and pulled it over your head. You moved your legs and arms slowly, like a reptile. I lifted you up and carried you into the kitchen just as your younger sister came in, barefoot and narrow-eyed with sleep.

'Good morning,' I said. 'Did you sleep well?'

She nodded. 'Can I hold her?'

'Yes, that would be great,' I said. 'Then I'll make her some milk. Here, sit on the bench.'

She sat down on the bench, and I handed you to her. While I filled the bright yellow electric kettle with water, got out the milk formula and the bottle, measured out six spoons and poured them into the lukewarm water, you half sat, half lay in her lap, kicking your feet.

'She's pretty happy, I think,' your sister said, taking your little fists in her own, which suddenly seemed big.

She was nine years old and given to thinking more about others than about herself, a character trait of hers that I had often wondered about, what had caused it. She had a light-filled soul, life flowed through her without encountering many obstacles, and maybe the fact that she didn't doubt herself, didn't question herself, somehow meant that what was her self didn't demand any effort or exertion, leaving plenty of space within her for other people. If I got angry with her and raised my voice even a little she reacted strongly, she began to cry so despairingly that I couldn't stand it and immediately tried to take it all back, usually in one of the many corners of the house which she sought out to be alone in her misery. But that almost never happened, firstly because she hardly ever did anything wrong, secondly because the consequences were so dire for her.

'Yes, that's good,' I said as I screwed the cap on, bent the soft rubber teat to the side with my thumb so the milk wouldn't squirt out and shook the bottle. In the eastern sky the red band had grown and the colour seemed to have become diluted, while the sky above it had paled. The ground, which stretched flatly away in every direction, hadn't begun to reflect the light, nor had the trees in the garden outside; on the contrary they seemed to suck it up, so that the blackness slowly filled with greyish grains, as if swollen with darkness.

'Do you want to feed her?' I said.

She nodded. 'But first I have to go to the loo.'

I took you on my arm and went into the living room, where your brother was lying on the sofa with a Mac in front of him, playing computer games. He was wearing green pyjamas that were too small for him, and his hair was tousled.

'So this is where you are,' I said. 'Have you been up a long time?'

'Yes,' he said, gazing at the screen.

'You know you're not allowed to play on the computer in the morning?'

'Yes,' he said.

He looked up at me and smiled. You peered at the lamp on the bookshelf.

'But there's nothing else to do,' he said.

'You can read,' I said.

'That's boring,' he said.

'Well, you can get dressed then,' I said and sat down. 'Or maybe you think that's boring too?'

'Yes,' he said, laughing. 'Everything is boring!'

I laid you on my lap with the back of your head resting against my knees, which I lifted so that you were almost sitting up, and met your gaze.

You flung out your arms and made a gurgling sound.

'What did you just think about?' I said.

You looked eagerly at me.

'Do you know what we're doing today?' I said.

You seemed to want to move your head, but didn't have full control over it, and it fell a little to the side.

'We're going to visit Mummy in Helsingborg,' I said. 'We'll drive there after we've taken the others to school.'

'I want to visit Mummy too,' your brother said, curling up next to us. You kept staring at me with wide-open eyes. We would sit like this a couple of times a day, it was a sort of exercise we did, and it had come about through fear, for when you were newborn I couldn't quite connect with you. The first month of your life you slept nearly the entire time, and when you weren't sleeping, you usually looked away. It was a trait I didn't recognise from your siblings; on the contrary I seemed to remember that they had met my gaze with open, curious eyes. I couldn't forget that contact, since it was as if I saw them then, the person they were, they seemed to emerge through their eyes. If their inner world was like a forest of undifferentiated sensations, these moments were like a glade within it, a sudden clearing. In your eyes I didn't see that, you were never quite present in your gaze, and it made me afraid. I thought something was wrong. I thought you might have brain damage or that you were autistic. I spoke to no one about this, for I believe that something becomes true if it is spoken. If it isn't spoken, it is as if it doesn't quite exist. And if it doesn't quite exist, it hasn't become fixed, and if it hasn't become fixed, it can still go away.

In other words, I shut my eyes against anything unpleasant. This was more than unpleasant, it was fateful.

You didn't look at us.

It lasted for a month. Then slowly you emerged, you became more and more present in the room and not just within yourself. And when I saw that, that you were emerging through your eyes, and that gradually there was even joy in them, my anxiety vanished. You were born a month early, and maybe that was why, maybe you needed those extra weeks to yourself. But the fright it gave me made me take extra care to speak to you, look at you, chat with you, fool around with you.

I had been afraid you might be brain damaged or autistic because your mother had been given some powerful medication at one time while she was expecting you. She had been in extreme distress, and the medication, which helped her, was adjusted to you too, so there was no real danger, but to be on the safe side you were delivered in a special ward and monitored for the first week. There were no signs that anything was wrong, you were perfectly sound and healthy, but still, that you avoided our gaze and preferred to look away when we tried to make eye contact was something I couldn't help worrying about.

On the other hand I knew how robust and strong infants are and how much it takes to disrupt their physiological life course. That the mother's varying states of mind might affect them, for instance, as they lay bobbing in the lukewarm water of the womb, I didn't believe in the slightest. Although they live in symbiosis with her, they are also autonomous, in the sense that the genetic codes determining their growth are fixed from the moment of conception.

People understood this in earlier times, I have sometimes thought. The old concept of fate expresses this too: that so much of what will happen has already been decided when the child is born.

'All of us are going to visit Mummy soon,' I said. 'But today you have to go to school.'

'What if I don't want to?' he said.

'Then I guess I'll have to carry you,' I said.

Just then your sister came in and sat down next to us, gentle and still a little sleepy in her movements.

'When you get home, Grandma will be here,' I said.

'She will?' your sister said.

'Yes!' your brother said, looking expectantly at me. 'Can I sleep in her bed?'

'I should think so,' I said. 'But tonight is Walpurgis night, remember? So you're probably going to stay up later than usual.'

'Is Grandma going to join us?'

'That I don't know,' I said and stood up. 'Could you hold her for a while? So I can go and have some coffee?'

Your sister nodded, and I laid you in the crook of her arm and handed her the bottle, which she immediately put in your mouth.

'You can come and get me if you need any help,' I said, looking at your brother. 'Can you handle that?'

'Of course,' your sister said, too focused on her task to look up at me.

'Come and get me if you need me,' I said again and went out into the kitchen, made myself a cup of coffee, carried it with me into the hall, stuck my feet in my shoes and opened the door. The cool spring air settled over my face like a film.

The sun had come up over the horizon. The blazing orange light, so clear and concentrated in the sky above, was dispersed by the sun's tremendous distance and seemed to have dissolved into the air down here, which was bright and light and fell over every surface, where it was reflected in soft colours, except where the rays of the sun shone directly, as on the top of the apple tree, where the half-unfurled leaves sparkled like little mirrors.

I walked across the yard to the house on the other side which I used as an office, and where I could smoke. It had been a workshop when we bought the property, and although I had covered every wall with books it still bore signs of its former use – in some indefinable way it seemed to have been fitted out to accommodate crude mechanical operations, connecting it to outdoor activities, rather like a garage, which neither the rugs on the floors nor the pictures on the walls could do more than gloss over.

I sat down in the chair in the corner. A pile of envelopes containing bills lay on the table next to it, they were my bad conscience, I never seemed to get around to paying them, and when I finally did it was always so late that reminders and debt collection notices had already been sent. It was so simple, all you had to do was pay, I had money, and yet it was only through huge exertion that I managed to get it done. On top of the pile lay a bill from Kronofogden, the Swedish Enforcement Authority, it was a serious matter, if the bill wasn't paid they would come knocking on our door. It had happened once while we were living in Malmö and once more since we moved here.

Oh!

I took the envelope, opened it, placed the bill on the table in front of me, turned on the Mac, went to the bank's home page, pulled the card case out of my back pocket and also placed it on the table while I looked around for the card reader. There it lay, on top of a book by William Blake on the book-shelf right next to where I was sitting. I inserted the card, typed the password, entered the code on the bank's home page, and was redirected to the page where bills were paid.

That done, I took a sip of coffee and got the pack of cig-arettes that was on the shelf below Blake, on top of a book by Sven Nykvist called *Vördnad för ljuset* (*In Reverence of the Light*) and one by Klaus Mann which I had never read. I had had these books for so long, and they had been standing in the same place for so many years, that I felt a familiarity with them more akin to the feeling one has for flowers in one's garden than for books. In both cases I contented myself with merely looking at them – there stood the lilies, there the Icelandic sagas, there stood the snowdrops, there Jayne Anne Phillips – and if I pulled out one of the books and began to read, it was like bringing the flowers inside and setting them in a vase.

Once I had been sitting at my desk working, I remem-bered now, when suddenly there was a thump behind me. I spun round. A book lay on the floor, it must have fallen from the bookshelf. But how? It had been standing on a perfectly flat shelf, held in place by other books. Curious, I got up and walked over to the shelf.

Could it have been an animal? A mouse or a rat?

No. For in the space left by the book that had fallen, there lay a creeper. It had grown along the outside wall of the house and up to the roof, where it had found a passage beneath the tiles and into the structure of the roof itself, between beams and boards, from which it had crept down along the inside wall of the room, encountered the bookshelf and pressed itself against the book, which was Bret Easton Ellis's novel *American Psycho*, and infinitely slowly pushed it along, millimetre by millimetre, until the day the book suddenly reached the point where gravity sucked it down and it fell to the floor two metres below with a loud thump.

I still found it incredible. And a little frightening, the blind force of growth; later, when I had got rid of the creepers and pulled them away from the wall like rope, fathom after fathom, I discovered that the parts that had grown below the roof were completely white, like everything that lives in darkness.

I leaned forward and tapped the little cap of ash on the cigarette against the rim of a cup. From where I was sitting I could see the other house, both the windows of the living room and the door, and imagine that I had some sort of oversight over what was going on in there. The minutes I managed to steal in this way, by letting your siblings look after you, felt exactly like that, stolen, unjustified. I knew it would be fine, that nothing dangerous would happen, so it was rather the feeling that it would look bad to others that bothered me as I leaned back in the chair, inhaled carefully so as not to set off another coughing fit, blew the smoke out and took another sip of coffee. What would happen if someone came here now and found me sitting in here smoking while I let young children look after a nearly newborn baby? What they would think?

Last summer, half a year before you were born, I had been summoned to a meeting with the Child Protection Service. It was a routine meeting, they always arranged one when it happened, the thing that had happened here, but it didn't leave me unaffected, and not just because it was humiliating to sit in an office answering questions from two young women, both of them in their twenties, about my children and about our life, but also because it was shameful, since it meant that we as a family had approached the zone where third parties had the right to get involved, had the right to give advice, even had the right to enter our lives and take over. Though it would never come to that, ultimately that was still what was at stake, that was the worst possible outcome of this meeting.

For this reason I didn't go as myself, I didn't go in there unwashed, with my hair messy and wearing the same clothes I had been using for weeks, as I normally did, it would be taking too great a risk, for then they would think I let the kids go unwashed too, with messy hair and clothes they had worn for weeks. No, that morning I showered, washed my hair, brushed my teeth, dressed in clean, presentable clothes, got in the car and drove to town.

It had been a marvellous summer, day after day of tall blue skies, still air, blazing sun, and this day was no different. As I parked the car, sunlight flooded the town, flashing off bonnets and roofs, windows and facades all around me, and though it was still early there were plenty of people in the streets, dressed in shorts and T-shirts, sleeveless tops and skirts, sandals and trainers. Even the air in the shade above the pavement outside the functionalist building where the meeting was to take place, right by the square, was warm and close.

I announced myself at reception and was told to sit down and wait. As in every waiting room there was a pile of weekly magazines on the table, and as almost always these days, at least in the places I had sat waiting, at medical centres, hospitals and car repair workshops, there were also a couple of free local newspapers. I picked up one of them, glanced at the date, it was several weeks old, but it didn't matter, for the news stories in it had the curious property of being completely empty, they didn't leave a single trace. When you had read them, it was exactly as if you hadn't.

Two young women entered the room. I stood up and shook their hands, they asked me to come with them to the floor above. There we went into a large room, they sat down on one side of a table, I on the other. They had documents in front of them. They said it was a matter of routine, they always did this when what had happened at our house happened. I said I understood and smiled at them, trying to seem as amiable and as normal as I could. Beneath the windows was a small park, I glanced for a moment at the motionless treetops, dense with light-filled leaves, the people walking by, the cars gleaming in the sunlight.

Then I looked briefly at the two women.

'Do you have children yourselves?' I said.

'No, unfortunately,' one of them said. The other shook her head and smiled.

So they didn't know anything, I thought, and felt annoyed that two people so young should question me about my family without having any experience of their own, without knowing anything beyond what they had read and been told about.

They asked me what had happened, and I told them.

Then they asked me to describe my children to them. I did, first I talked about the eldest one, then the middle one and finally about the youngest. I knew they wanted to assure themselves that I was in touch with my children, that I 'saw' them, who they were, and I tried as best I could to give them what they wanted, even though it went against the grain, precisely because they didn't have children of their own and couldn't relate what I was saying to anything they had experienced personally. At the same time I was nervous, I fumbled for words, I felt what I was saying was inadequate and revealing.

One of them seemed to be suppressing a smile as I talked.

Was I being ridiculous in any way?

Was there something wrong with the way I talked about my children?

Suddenly my eyes grew moist.

I looked away, to cry here was the worst thing I could do, then they would write 'unstable' or 'unsuited' in their papers. 'Father emotionally unstable.'

'It's not easy to describe them,' I said. 'They are so many things.'

'We understand that,' one of them said and smiled.

'Who is looking after them now?' said the other.

'Two friends who are visiting us,' I said. 'They're a couple. They have three children of their own. Three grown-up children. The youngest one just moved out recently.'

'Well, that sounds good,' one of them said. They both smiled.

The meeting lasted no more than half an hour and nothing happened, yet I was shaken when I came out into the street again. The shocking thing lay in the service's name, that the children might need to be protected by someone other than us. Yes, maybe even need to be protected *against* us.

Since then every emotional outburst by the children, all the mess in our house, all the disarray in our affairs has led my thoughts to the Child Protection Service, as if we were living on a knife edge.

My reason told me it wasn't really like this, but the image still had me in its power: we were living on a knife edge.

Even a little thing like having a beer in the evening was unthinkable. I imagined an unannounced home visit, with me sitting in the sofa drinking while I was in charge of three young children.

But the children were completely unaware. At times I thought that my job was taking care of the shadows, so that they would grow up in the light. That I devoured shadows.

They must have sensed something, though. There were some shadows I couldn't absorb. And perhaps I myself was like a shadow to them.

I dropped the still burning cigarette into one of the cups on the table, where it went out with a short, faint hiss, stood up and walked back to the house.

When I took your brother and younger sister to the day-care centre a while later, you lay in the pram gazing up at the luminous blue sky. The way there ran right across the yard of the neighbouring farm – between an enormous brick building that was partly a stable, partly a barn, and the farm-house, which lay back a little from the road beneath a cluster of leafy trees – and down along a dirt road lined with trees on one side and wide fields on the other. In winter we walked in the dark, far from the first light of day which might appear as a pale ribbon on the horizon, and if the sky was cloudless it felt as if we were in the middle of the universe somewhere, among stars and planets, while during the summer half of the year the light seemed to heighten whatever was here, the fields and the trees, the soil and the grass, growing denser and richer the closer we got to midsummer.

Now there was still something frugal about it all, the landscape lacked the deep fullness that came with summer, the green of the trees was still merely a tinge, for that is April: buds, shoots, uncertainty, hesitation. April lies between the great sleep and the great leap. April is the longing for something else, where the object of longing is still unknown.

With one hand I pushed the pram across the open space between the buildings, holding your brother's hand in the other, he was nearly seven and could still hold hands with his father without giving it a thought, while your sister walked on the other side, their school bags dangling on their backs. I really wanted them to walk to school on their own, as I had at their age, but now, in these circumstances, I was afraid the staff would think this was out of laziness, that I neglected them, therefore I walked with them every morning the few hundred metres down to the building where the day-care centre was located.

We reached the top of the ridge, from which we could see the fields extending towards some gentle hills in the distance. Some areas were yellow, those were rapeseed fields, some were green, some were a dry brown, they had been ploughed not long ago. Everything shone in the light of the low, blazing sun.

'When are you picking us up today, Dad?' your sister said.

'I don't know,' I said. 'Maybe around four?'

'Dad is visiting Mum,' your brother said.

'I miss Mum,' your sister said.

'I know,' I said. 'She misses you too.'

'And me?' your brother said.

'Yes, of course she does!' I said.

I had always known that they loved her more than me, or with greater intensity. She was warmer and more sincere than I was, and gave them something I couldn't. And yet they needed me too, for when I came home after having been away, it was as if something calmed down within them, and in the house too, as if my presence created a kind of balance in their lives.

The jostling of the pram had made your eyelids heavy, and when we stopped outside the yellow building, part of which was used as a kind of café for the elderly, you were asleep. I let you lie in the pram and followed the others inside to show my face to the staff. One of them was going into the inner room, where five or six children were seated around two tables, waiting, pushing a trolley of milk cartons, yoghurt and breakfast cereals.

'Hi there,' I said.

'Hi,' she said.

Your sister and brother had already taken off their shoes and coats. Your sister squeezed herself hastily against me before she followed her brother in, and as always I wondered whether she did it for my sake or for her own.

'Bye then!' I said and watched them slide into their chairs and seem to merge with the other children, subdued now in the early morning, with no further ties to me. A similar thing happened to me as soon as I shut the door behind me: the children disappeared from my consciousness, the entire day might pass without me giving them a thought, until they returned to my mind late in the afternoon when it was time to pick them up again.

Outside you were still asleep. I released the brake of the pram with my foot, opened the iron gate with one hand, pulled the pram through, closed the gate again and started down the narrow tarmacked path towards the road, which we followed for maybe twenty metres before turning off onto the dirt road.

The trees that grew close to the road, almost like a wall, were part of a small forest, a square-shaped area between the large housing development where the majority of the village's inhabitants lived, and the older part of the village around the church, where we lived. There was a big dilapidated brick mansion in there, and a pond I assumed must be artificial, and the whole thing was surrounded by a fence, so it was probably an old park or a large garden rather than a forest. There was something dark and gloomy about the place, the ground seemed waterlogged and lay permanently in shadow, but once, I thought, this must have been the centre of something, where money flowed in and was spent. Perhaps it belonged to the church and was in fact the parsonage?

Some decades ago there had been a brewery in the village, and a dairy, several shops and workshops, a bank and a post office, and trains had stopped here, but as farming became mechanised during the 1960s and 70s, all secondary activities came to a halt and people began to move away. Now there was just a grocery shop left, and it would probably fold when the current owners retired, the woman who worked there had said once. The old school closed down the first year we lived here, the kindergarten had difficulty attracting enough children to stay in business.

In between the trees, in a small glade, a huge horse stood peering at us. The shaggy hair around its fetlocks made it look like it was wearing fur boots. It was probably an Ardennes horse, I had concluded. The sun fell across its broad back and down along its bulging, muscular flank. It gazed at us calmly and thoughtfully for a while before it bowed its head and continued grazing, while I walked up towards the crest of the low ridge, pushing the pram where you lay sleeping, as a man in a boiler suit came out of the farmhouse, crossed the yard and climbed into a pickup. I lifted my hand, and he returned the greeting. Though we were neighbours we had never exchanged a single word beyond hello, and I knew nothing about him. It had to do with orientation, his house – Did he live there alone? Did he have a wife? Kids? – lay behind ours, and while we related to the road out front and the link to the city that it represented, closely connected to the world flowing in through the fibre-optic cables and appearing to us on our TV and computer screens, his house was out back, facing the fields and meadows, which he presumably also farmed, a reality that lay outside my experience and had left its mark on the land-scape with its ancient structures – wide fields with small clusters of houses around a church. We lived right in the middle of it and I saw it every day, field after field, village after village, church after church, yet I still longed for it, at times intensely. What was it I longed for? To be connected with it through something other than my gaze, perhaps.

In other words, with my body? To work on the land? The few times in my life I had done that, I had longed to get away, to go back inside into the warmth, to my books or the television.

This wasn't entirely true. In the past few years I had worked in the garden at regular intervals, and after the bore-dom and resistance of the first couple of hours I seemed to pass through a wall, to fall into a rhythm and become pos-sessed by it, not stopping until it was nearly midnight.

But for God's sake, that was just a garden!

The garden was a small, artificial, pretend world, nature in it was pretend nature, and it lacked necessity, nothing was created there other than a sense of inner satisfaction, which was no doubt a pretend satisfaction, since it derived from something artificial.

The light of the rising sun gave the bricks of the shed in front of us a reddish glow. On the road which lay maybe a hundred metres beyond and ran straight through the village, an articulated lorry passed, big as a small house. The deep drone of the engine seemed to hang trembling in the air beneath the cawing of the jackdaws which nested in the tree-tops in a corner of the gloomy estate, and I suddenly remembered the special sound produced by the Volvos of the 1970s. Besides the hum of the engine and the rushing noise of the tyres against the tarmac they made a kind of thin, high-pitched, almost whiny sound, like that of a small flute. When we walked along the upper road in the housing development, out of sight of the main road which ran maybe ten metres below, I could always tell whether or not the passing car was a Volvo.

I turned off the path behind the stable, pushed the pram across the neighbour's lawn and into our back garden, through the gate and over to the door, where I positioned it so that I could see you from the window, then walked into the hall.

'Are you awake?' I shouted.

Upstairs, your sister grunted something or other.

'You have to get up now,' I said. 'The bus leaves in half an hour!'

'Okaaaay,' she said.

'Now!'

'OK! I said OK!'

'Good! Well, come on then.'

'Oh, Dad! Stop it!'

I went into the kitchen, put two slices of bread in the toaster, turned on the electric kettle, got out the margarine, some cheese and a packet of sliced ham from the fridge, put it all on a tray and carried it into the room where the dining table stood just as your sister came down the stairs, with the duvet wrapped around her like a kind of cape, and walked past me into the living room without meeting my gaze.

'Do you want some tea?' I said.

'No, thanks,' she said.

'I've already put the kettle on.'

'So why did you ask?'

'You have a point there,' I said and walked over to the window to see if you were still asleep. You were. I went back into the kitchen, took a tea bag from the box, got a cup and dropped the bag into it, then poured in the steaming water.

'Well, come and eat,' I said when I had carried the cup and saucer out and set it down at her place at the table.

'I'm not hungry,' she said from the living room.

'You have to eat at least one slice.'

I went over and stood in the door opening. She was lying on the sofa with the duvet over her. The room was dim, the sun was on the other side of the house, but the road outside, grey and dry, was lit here and there by its rays, wherever they passed unobstructed between trees and hedges, house walls and bushes.

'Pardon me, miss,' I said. 'The bus leaves in twenty minutes. You're not even dressed.'

'That's plenty of time.'

'If you start now, it is. Your baby sister is sleeping in the pram outside. Do you think you could keep an eye on her? And tell me if she wakes up?'

She looked up at me suspiciously.

'Where are you going?'

'To the loo.'

'That's more information than I asked for,' she said.

'That's exactly the information you asked for!' I said.

I could see she was trying to hide a smile.

'But could you?'

'Oh all right then,' she said, sitting up. 'But I won't drink the tea.'

I entered the bathroom, locked the door behind me, pulled down my trousers and sat down on the toilet seat. The white curtain, which my mother had crocheted for us, was filled with light. A shadow looking like a long neck with a small head bobbed faintly back and forth across it as the piss splashed against the porcelain and trickled down towards the water at the bottom of the bowl. It was as if the curtain absorbed the rays of the sun completely, for the white light appeared to come from the material itself, as if it were lit from within. Every object in here, such as the two large bars of soap that lay on the shelf beneath the changing table, ready to be grabbed by whoever was in the bath, one light blue, almost turquoise, the other sand-coloured, still with the brand name etched on the surface, or the little stack of folded flannels next to them, appeared to rest in itself, as if independently of the light, which was so discreet and so evenly distributed throughout the room that it seemed invisible, and yet it was the light that made everything stand out. The plastic bottles of shampoo and conditioner, white with green caps, the blue plastic bag bulging with nappies, the toothbrushes in the cup on the sink, red, white, yellow, green, blue. All these objects were not just lying there, they made up the room. It was easy to think of the room as essentially an empty cube that had been filled with things, but that room existed only in our minds, it belonged to our way of thinking. All painters possessed this knowledge, that's why one of the first things they learned was to draw not the objects but the spaces between them. They learned how to relate to space in a way that wasn't obvious. Even a bathroom, visited several times a day and more familiar than any other place, is held together by an assumption about reality, and can, if one makes an effort and resists the perception of the room created by that assumption, turn into if not exactly a wilderness, then at least something chaotic, a monstrous accumulation of forms and patterns, colours and planes.

But why would one?

I contracted my abdominal muscles and felt the stool sliding through the final stretch of the intestine, where it had been accumulating as more and more waste arrived, not unlike a sausage being stuffed, and out through my anus.

The most bestial thing about it wasn't so much the faint flare of satisfaction it gave me as the fact that it smelled good. I have always thought that there is something pre-civilised about this, that our own stool has a mild and pleasant smell, while everyone else's smells terrible.

I stood up, tore off a strip of toilet paper and wiped myself. As I was about to drop the paper into the bowl to flush it down, I saw that it was full of blood.

Pale red streaks ran down the white porcelain, while the blood at the bottom was darker, heavier somehow.

Blood? And so much of it?

Blood meant danger, and I became frightened.

But then I thought, whatever happens happens.

It was a good thought.

I glanced around quickly, although I knew there was no one else in there, pushed the button on the cistern and watched as fresh, clear water flowed down the sides flushing the used, red water away through the waste pipe. Then I pulled up my trousers, washed my hands under the tap, dried them on the towel hanging beside the sink. It was probably just haemorrhoids, I thought – I sat still all day and had done so for years – it was nothing to worry about.

But my father's father had died of internal bleeding, hadn't he? He had thought it was haemorrhoids and hadn't gone to see a doctor, and then Grandmother had found him on the bathroom floor, and when he arrived at the hospital it became clear that the loss of blood had been massive.

But was that what he died of?

No, he lived for a while after that.

So what did he die of then?

I thought of what my grandmother had said when she told me about the incident. He was lying on the bathroom floor, weak and close to death, they waited for the ambulance, and he had taken her hand and then he had said that they would go for a holiday in the sun. Maybe he said it to comfort her, to give her courage in the midst of uncertainty, and maybe she squeezed his hand and said yes, they would. But to us, my brother and me, she had said, laughing, that he was probably heading for a hotter place than the Mediterranean.

It was a good comment, and I'm sure I smiled, but inside I felt chilled to the core.

Now I unlocked the door and went into the dining room, where your elder sister was sitting at the table with a half-eaten slice of bread on the plate in front of her.

'About time!' she said.

'You're the one who's late, not me,' I said. 'You'll have to get dressed now if we're going to make it.'

'She hasn't woken up,' she said.

'It's good for her to sleep outside,' I said.

'Why?'

'Fresh air. It's healthy. But thanks for looking after her.'

I took the phone out of my pocket and checked the time.

'The bus leaves in eleven minutes,' I said.

'But I haven't finished eating.'

'Bring the sandwich with you. Come along, now.'

She looked as if she was about to protest, then she thought better of it, stood up and walked towards the bathroom, closing the door behind her.

I sat down at the table. The pram outside was flooded with light, the metal handle sparkled, but your face lay in shadow, and though the white bonnet wrapped around your head made you resemble a flower bulb, there was something dignified about you as you slept, something almost majestic: you looked as if the world belonged to you.

And so it did.

I felt a stab of joy in my chest and stood up, gathered up the dirty plates and carried them into the kitchen, put them in the dishwasher. I suppose I should see a doctor, I thought, looking out at the garden through the window, at the grass which was still pale green, the scattered blue flowers glowing on the lawn beneath the apple tree. But that was one of the things I didn't do. There was something embarrassing about getting myself examined by a doctor only to find that nothing was wrong.

The door opened again, and your sister came marching out with a hairbrush lifted to her head.

'OK, let's go,' I said, glancing at the clock.

The bus was leaving in seven minutes.

Ever since she was as small as you are now, your elder sister has taken in everything that went on around her, and ever since then I have wondered whether her great sensitivity was something that came in addition, something she had more of than others, or whether it came about because she had less of whatever it was that in most people kept the world at a distance. If a lot happened in one day, if we had gone for a long walk around town with the pram, she would start to cry when we got home, sometimes inconsolably. When she was a little older, she would sometimes close her eyes and pretend to be asleep in the pram if we ran into someone we knew, or hide if we had visitors at home. These were an infant's methods of parrying events.

Oh, what a difference there is between simply being in the world, as if immune to all its impressions, and being defenceless and taking everything in. If one is protected, then one is free, then one can do whatever one feels like doing. Back then I noticed a lot of children who seemed to be clad in a protective emotional suit, shielding them from all the millions of impressions, impulses and wills that operated between people, and who without the least inhibition banged toy cars on the floor, ran shouting through rooms or were simply present in a room with such unquestioned naturalness that they shone like miniature suns. Your siblings only behaved like this in places where they felt completely safe, where they had been many times and where they knew everyone. So for us a lot revolved around doing the same things every day, creating a sense of stability and safety.

There's a reason why it's called the nuclear family. For when your siblings were at the so-called obstinate age when a child begins to assert its own will, when emotions flow freely and every little thing can become an insurmountable obstacle, and stability and consistency are especially important, or later, during episodes when feelings got out of control, a chain reaction might occur in which their actions snagged on mine and finally made me explode in ways I hadn't experienced since I myself was a child, when my vision could suddenly cloud with anger. Even when we were among other people I sometimes lost my temper completely. Once I roared THAT'S ENOUGH! THAT'S ENOUGH! to your elder sister in the middle of a shopping centre, she was maybe two and a half years old, and I slung her over my shoulder and carried her like a sack out to the street while she screamed and kicked and I fumed inwardly. Obviously people stared, I let them stare, I was in a place where other people and their opinions didn't matter. Afterwards, wild regrets, wild despair. If I knew anything about raising children, it was that predictability was crucial. And that the first years of a child's life were decisive for the later development of its personality. So what was I doing? I hardly recognised myself. The last time I had been angry was in my early twenties. My mother would sometimes say that I suffered from inhibited aggression, but I thought the reason she said this was that she herself was inhibited, for that's how it is, the traits that are easiest for us to identify in others are those that predominate in ourselves. In my own eyes I was a calm person. I never got angry at others even when I had reason to, for instance when someone humiliated me. This was because I turned the guilt inwards, turned the rage inwards, towards myself, not because I wanted to but because that's how I was. Every train of thought that I had before falling asleep at night ended in something either shameful or in a strong sense of guilt, and when the thought ended there, I had a mental image of shooting myself, with the barrel stuck into my mouth or aimed at my temple or my forehead, before I tried to think of something else, which after a few moments would end up in the same image, of me shooting myself. This became so habitual that I didn't even notice it. The first time I did, I tried to make it stop, but I couldn't, the image had become reflexive. In my mind I stuck the barrel into my mouth or aimed it at my temple, my forehead, I couldn't help it. Nor was I able to direct the aggression outwards instead, it was impossible to aim the imagined weapon at some imaginary other, I just couldn't do it, not even in my thoughts was I able to lay a finger on anyone but myself. And why should I? They had nothing to do with me.

That's why it was strange to feel the rage coursing through my body again during those years, as if an old dead tree were to feel the sap rising once more. It was so far removed from the person I thought I was. Was *this* me? Had my rage lain dormant all these years? And did other emotions lie dormant too, ready to erupt as soon as the conditions were right? Were we ruled by circumstances, did they bring out the person we really were?

One time I got so angry that I smashed my fist as hard as I could against the armrest of the sofa, which broke, while your two sisters stared wide-eyed at me.

I was gnawed by the worry that this had stayed with them, in the form of cracks in their self-esteem, cracks in their self-confidence. On the other hand there were so many days, and so much of the time we spent together there was no drama. And then so much of what small children need is of a practical nature – all the meals, all the changes of clothing, all the trips outdoors, and then there was the kindergarten, which was also run according to rules and where order prevailed, so that in the midst of the inward chaos there was an outer balance, a system, a space, a hope, a light. It worked, your siblings grew up, and I liked to think that they were neither better nor worse off than other children, for every family has its problems, mine did and yours does and every other family I know; it is part of the condition of our lives.

But maybe these were just excuses, something I said to comfort myself. For that's how it is, we cover up our mistakes and failings, we invent stories that put ourselves in a more favourable light. Self-deception is perhaps the most human thing of all.

In the course of these years I also came to understand that it wasn't as I had always thought previously – that the child developed while the parents remained the same, that the child grew up under an unchanging regime – but that the relationship was much more dynamic, that the child to some extent created its own upbringing. This was because a child's differing needs had to be fulfilled in different ways, as if the parents' thoughts and actions were a river that adjusted itself to the child's course, filling it in places where before there was nothing, flowing past where it was full.

Your elder sister was proud and afraid, she tossed her head and no one could silence her, she was still a child but had the irony of an adult, it helped her to keep the world at a distance. If the distance became too great, closeness had to be reinforced, and it was the same way with security, for if feeling secure simply meant that she avoided every challenge, turning away from it, then it would keep her from developing. If this didn't happen on its own, at least it occurred without planning, and through all the thousands of small daily adjustments that were made in order to make everything flow as easily and effortlessly as possible, patterns were created, eddies, ways of being, both in the children and in the parents.

But this year the entire focus had been on survival.

I pushed the pram over to the car, lifted you up, and you opened your eyes, but you didn't cry, you hardly ever did, you just looked about you as if you let yourself be filled with whatever was there, thinking, *So this is where I am now.* I pulled the sliding door of the car aside, supported myself with one hand, held you tight with the other and climbed up, placed you gently into the baby seat, fastened the straps. Then I took the pram apart and put it in the boot, before hurrying in to get the bag with nappies, wet wipes, a change of clothing and milk, which was standing ready in the hall, as your sister headed towards the car holding her satchel. There were no more backpacks in her world; everyone had satchels, she had said, so we gave her one.

As I started the car, three minutes remained until the bus left.

'Will we make it?' your sister asked.

'We'll find out,' I said, leaning forward to see around the hedge as we rolled slowly out of the driveway with the tyres crunching on the gravel.

Up above the fields the blades of the wind turbines turned slowly beneath the vast, pale blue sky.

I sped up towards the crossroads, blinked my left indicator, all clear, and we turned into the street that ran between the community hall and the fire station over towards the edge of the mysterious, waterlogged and overgrown estate, to the big, sprawling, still not densely leafy trees where the flocks of jackdaws stayed at night, where I again hit the brakes before a crossroads, this one with the highway.

'Are you coming with us to Walpurgis tonight?' I said.

'Go watch a bonfire? No, thanks.'

'You liked it when you were small,' I said, driving out onto the road.

'Do I look small to you now?'

'Not really.'

'Exactly,' she said and looked out the window. The pavement outside was covered with autumn leaves, leathery brown rags which didn't seem to have anything in common with the fresh, pale green leaves that had begun to appear on the branches above them.

She looked at me again. 'When are you picking me up?'

'I don't know,' I said. 'But not super-early.'

'Two?'

'Ha ha.'

'Then three.'

'We'll see.'

At the end of the big hedge we turned left again. The bus left in one minute, but we would make it easily, for now we saw it standing at the end of the road, outside the day-care centre, with lights blinking and a line of children waiting to enter.

'So, let's say three o'clock.'

'I can't promise you that,' I said.

'Yes, you can,' she said.

We passed the row of single-storey yellow-brown brick houses, all of them with little gardens that glowed green in the sunlight, in between the flashing metal and glass, pulled in ahead of the bus, turned in the car park and stopped next to the line of kids, which was rapidly diminishing as one by one they climbed into the bus.

Your sister opened the door. 'Three o'clock,' she said.

'Have a nice day today,' I said.

'Dad! Three!'

'I'll try,' I said and watched as she walked over to the others and stood last in line, a head taller than the rest.

I got out my phone and turned it on. A message had arrived, it was from a neighbour, he wanted to know if we could have coffee. I replied that I'd be there in five minutes, and as the bus headed down the road, heavy and slow like a large old animal, I put the phone in my pocket, put the car in gear and turned into the road.

'Are you OK back there?' I said as I glanced in the mirror, though I could only see the baby seat – you were sitting almost banana-shaped in it, with your head well below the top.

You didn't answer the question, not even with a gurgle or another of your many sounds. I imagined that you were gazing at the sky and the trees along the road, and at the tops of the houses, and, at the bottom of the gentle slope, perhaps also at the upper part of the road and the cars that must be up there. Everything slid into you, while in the quiet of your mind you were perhaps labouring to keep things separate in a more fundamental way than my thoughts did. Perhaps joy flowed through you when you saw the sky, since you recognised it and recognition to you was a good thing?

O sky, O sun, O green meadow!

Oh, you sweet innocent child!

We drove past the grocery shop, which hadn't opened yet but where one could knock and be allowed in even if one came early or too late, we drove past the old car repair workshop, and the Thai restaurant was in front of us as I turned left and we rolled past the sports ground on one side and the long row of houses forming the end of the large housing development where most of the village residents lived on the other. The neighbour we were going to visit lived in a house in the middle of a field between two villages. It had originally belonged to the Church, presumably a major landowner in the area at one time. The gravel road leading to it was a few hundred metres long, full of holes which in autumn and winter were usually filled with water, but which now, after the dry weather of the past weeks, lay like empty grey craters.

'You haven't fallen asleep, have you?' I said, keeping to the very edge of the road as we drove across the fields, which were partly green with new shoots, partly brown with recently ploughed soil.

The neighbour was standing at his door as we turned in through the fairly narrow passage between the houses and entered the yard, swung around the small newly planted tree in the middle and parked.

'How are things?' he said as I climbed out.

'Pretty good,' I said. 'How about yourself?'

'Oh all right,' he said. 'You want some coffee?'

'Sure,' I said, glancing through the car window to check whether you were asleep. You were.

He had moved here with his partner and their son a year and a half ago. Their son had become best friends with your brother, and when I drove him over here, I would have coffee in their kitchen. He made documentaries, wrote books and had worked as a journalist for many years. He was a restless, friendly soul, and there was hardly anywhere in the world he hadn't been. His partner was an artist and was now working on a documentary about her grandmother, who one evening after the war had shot two of her children and then herself in a villa in Bromma outside Stockholm. Her father had grown up in the shadow cast by that incident, and through him, I assumed, so had she.

'Nice weather today,' he said. 'Almost like summer.'

'Yes,' I said, looking up at him standing there on the stairs with his head lifted towards the sun. He wore an elegant scarf tied around his neck, a thin burgundy-coloured sweater and dark brown baggy suit trousers, for that's how he was, the shabby and the elegant went hand in hand, together with the upright and the slumped, the resolute and the hesitant, the cheerful and the anxious. Standing there on the stairs with his head lifted towards the sun, he was erect and radiated a kind of natural mild authority, whereas when we entered the kitchen and he began making coffee, there was something uncertain and feeble about his body language, his neck was bent, his back was bowed, his hands slowly and hesitantly disassembled the coffee maker as if he had only a faint recollection of how it was done.

You don't know what personality is, and I hardly know myself, for it is a strange phenomenon, but it has to do with the sum of all the traits a person has, the totality they form, which is what people around them relate to when they meet or think about him or her. Personality resides within the individual in the form of thoughts, feelings and will, which are not initially abstract entities but rather founded upon something startlingly concrete: the traces left by reactions in the brain when different cells communicate with each other. What a person wants can change radically, for example after brain surgery, if healthy cells have been removed, or as a result of traumatic brain injury, and so can all other personality traits, so that a previously calm and humble person may become irascible and rude, a considerate person may become selfish, a prude may become vulgar. The people in his or her close circle of acquaintances will immediately notice the change, but not the person themselves, since he or she will not have access to their previous personality and therefore no point of comparison. The frightening thing about this is that it seems to be entirely arbitrary what personality one has; one is oneself and lives one's life regardless, even if one is suddenly endowed with a brand new and entirely different personality.

So what is personality? Is it like a vessel within which the self exists, full of little walls, partitions and hatches, which the self fills up and never gets beyond, until a possible accident or illness alters the walls, partitions and hatches, so that the self settles in a new way, into a new form?

Since thoughts, emotions and will can be controlled to a certain extent, perhaps even governed, it is surprising that personality is apparently so stable throughout one's life, so consistent and predictable. We rarely experience people we know going wild, doing or saying something that takes us completely by surprise, which we had never expected of them. Furthermore, it is surprising that the variations between different personalities are so minor that we are never really curious, when we meet a new person, as to what in the world this person might take it into their head to say or do, but always take it for granted that they will be more or less like us.

This must be so because we are formed in each other's image yet are not ourselves aware of this, since personality reigns supreme within the individual, no one has two personalities, or three, and this supremacy, the unique standing that personality has in the individual, makes us unable to see the extent to which it has been formed by other personalities, and that in reality we are like a flock of birds, or a pack of wolves, or a troop of monkeys.

If personality is a result of certain reaction patterns in the brain, and if these could be traced in the form of images, then perhaps the patterns would resemble trees, which are made up of the same elements, trunk, branches, crown, bark, leaves, and which develop according to the surrounding conditions, the quality of the soil, the amount of light, whether they are sheltered from the wind or not, so that every tree grows into a unique shape, with branches pointing up or down, a trunk that is stunted or erect, but at the same time they all resemble each other and together form a forest.

That was Bazarov's image of mankind, that people are like trees in a forest, and that we are so much alike that our individual differences are insignificant. A heart is a heart, a brain is a brain, a mouth is a mouth.

But you don't know who Bazarov is either!

He is a character in the Russian author Turgenev's novel *Fathers and Sons*, and has come to be seen as the very incarnation of nihilism. Actually he is a materialist and a realist – only what can be measured and counted has value – and a cynic, his best one-liner in the novel is when he says, I look up to heaven only when I want to sneeze. *Fathers and*

*Sons* is about how cynicism, which only acknowledges the tangible, is ground to dust when Bazarov experiences that which isn't tangible but which still exists, and which triumphs over free will, namely love, which in his case manifests itself as an obsession. The woman he wants, Anna Odintsova, has never loved anyone, and she rejects him. The scene in which it happens is strange, they are up in her room on the first floor, it is dark outside and the room is dim, and the air between them is rife with tension. Strange because it is so clearly a case of love, which since it has arisen between two loveless people appears as something alien, something almost extrapersonal, which fills them even as they are unable to relate to it.

What is love then, when it forces its way against the will? When it is unwanted but still takes over? Does it come from a place beyond personality, as wind comes from outside the tree which bends under its force? Or does it only come from somewhere beyond consciousness? For consciousness can be directed, it can be shaped by ideals and notions as it suits us. Feelings on the other hand cannot be directed, at least not the most powerful of them, but they can be explained in ways we find convenient.

After Bazarov has been unmanned by love and his love has been rejected, he goes to his parents. It turns out that they love their only son with all their heart and soul. This all-encompassing love, which resembles idolatry and which accepts everything, even rejection, is depicted as good, while Bazarov's rejection of it is portrayed as heartless. And it is heartbreaking to read about how he hurts his good and lovable parents, for whom he is the centre of life. Is he a bad person?

What is a bad person?

Am I a bad person?

Was my father a bad person?

My father's mother, was she a bad person?

Turgenev set his novel exactly at the intersection between that within us which we can control and that which we cannot, and even though Bazarov, who is young and inexperienced, has chosen cynicism and disillusionism, he hasn't chosen the forces that motivate his choice. His parents' love is suffocating, and for someone who grows up in the midst of it, everything will hinge on resisting it in order to become one's own person. To break the bonds, turn one's back, reject. Then it won't take much for every emotion to be greeted with suspicion, including one's own.

Is it that simple? That cruelty comes from either too much or too little love?

Perhaps in a novel it is that simple, for novels are written to elucidate some aspect of human life, so that something which exists but perhaps lacks form is given a form and becomes visible.

Life has no such form.


What your personality was like no one knew yet, not even you, but certain traits had begun to appear, for example that you were calm, that you were robust, that you were sunny.

The neighbour, on the other hand, who had lived for nearly sixty years, was restless, not very robust, rather evasive, which was perhaps a way to counter the robustness he lacked, and though he seemed mild, I had a feeling that when pushed to the limit he could be hard and capable of being ruthless. I don't know why I thought that. With me he had never been anything but friendly. He was sensitive to others, as certain trees are more sensitive to wind, and he was curious, perhaps more about phenomena and events than about people, since they didn't get as close to him. But the most noticeable thing about him was that he seemed to need people around him, that he couldn't stand being alone for long periods. He would gladly walk the three kilometres to my house for a cup of coffee and a chat, even if what was said wasn't particularly interesting, and without demanding or expecting intimacy, it seemed that all he wanted was someone, it hardly mattered who, to sit and talk with.

Now he was standing with his back to me. He spooned coffee into the filter, screwed on the top of the coffee maker, placed it on the hotplate and switched on the heat. I turned round and saw through the window that you were still asleep in the back seat of the car.

'The Russians have been active lately,' he said and sat down on the other side of the big wooden table. What had to be the remains of yesterday's dinner was still on the table, three dishes smeared with congealed sauce, two pots, glasses half filled with stale, greyish water. The kitchen counter on the other side was also full of dirty dishes. A strongly anti-bourgeois attitude to life was evident in their home, keeping things tidy was not a priority, so every room was a cluttered mess. Our house was the same way, but it gave me a bad conscience, and I always struggled against it. I didn't get the impression that he did.

'What are you thinking of?' I said.

'All the overflights. That they've started to violate Swedish airspace.'

'Norway's too,' I said.

'The bear is stirring,' he said. 'It's interesting.'

I got out my cigarettes and lit one, noticed him glancing at the pack and held it out to him.

'I suppose I could have one,' he said.

As he lit it, he sucked on the cigarette as if it were a cigar, holding his arms close to his forward-leaning torso, but as soon as it was lit, he leaned back in the chair and flung out the hand holding the smoking cigarette in a generous gesture, like a man of the world.

'The EU should never have attempted to get closer to the Ukraine,' he said. 'Then you haven't understood much about Russia and Russian history.'

'What do you mean?'

'Well, Kiev was the first great city in what became the Russian empire. In the early Middle Ages, when Moscow was just a small village. The Ukraine and Russia are like twins. Or at least close relatives. They belong together. At least the Russians see it that way.'

'Yes,' I said.

'What has held Russia together has always been the state, not Russian culture, and the state has always been expansive. No other country has had more fluid national borders than Russia throughout its history. The Ukraine has been inside and outside it countless times. The very idea of Russia is imperialistic.'

'I know nothing about Russian history,' I said. 'But I just read a novel by Turgenev, *Smoke*, it's terribly melodramatic, but anyway in it they speak about Russia and Russianness and about the relationship to Europe. I think it's set in the 1850s. But the things they say might have been said today.'

'Exactly,' he said and stood up, still with the cigarette in his hand, which he held out into the air as he walked over to the stove and pressed the coffee maker against the hotplate. The water began to hiss.

'How much time do you have?' he asked.

'Not that much, actually,' I said. 'I'm going up to Helsingborg.'

'How is she?'

'Pretty good,' I said. 'She's probably coming home soon.'

I turned and looked out the window again. You had woken up, and you were crying.

I stood up.

'She's woken up,' I said.

'Oh well,' he said.

'I'll bring her in here for a little while then.'

'Go ahead,' he said.

You were still crying as I opened the door and climbed into the car. I loosened the seat belt and lifted you up, pressed you close to my chest, got out the carton of milk and the baby bottle, a little stressed out that you were so upset, unscrewed the top with one hand, held you with the other, carefully poured the milk into the bottle, screwed the top back on, carried you into the kitchen, put you on my lap with your head on my arm, and stuck the bottle into your mouth. You instantly stopped screaming and started to suck. I undid the knot under your chin and took off your cap, ran my fingers through your thin reddish-blonde hair, felt how incredibly soft your scalp was. The neighbour placed a cup in front of me and poured coffee into it.

'I guess she was hungry,' he said.

'Looks that way,' I said and lifted the coffee cup in an arc around your face while you sucked eagerly and greedily at the bottle like a little lamb.

A muffled, distant roar sounded outside. Then another.

'Is there an exercise going on?'

'Yes. I suppose they're running a little scared,' he said, smiling.

The Swedish military had an artillery range down at Kabusa, on the slopes leading down to the sea. When it wasn't in use, it was open to the public. I had taken walks there several times, along the paths down to the beaches, a windblown, grass-covered area which in the summer could be almost unbearably beautiful, on days when the air stood motionless in the heat, when the sun went down in the west and the sea lay perfectly still and glittering, and the big metal discs that had been set up here and there, full of bullet holes, seemed like objects from another, alien culture, even more alien than the archaic circle of stones from the Viking age that stood on a grassy plateau a few kilometres further north.

There was another boom. It was a beautiful, hypnotic sound. As from some somnambulant force, something non-human, deep within the world.

'If the Russians should take it into their minds to invade, this is where they'd come,' he said.

'Well, that would be exciting,' I said. 'Shake things up a little.'

We had a mutual friend in the village, he was a writer and a sociologist, and after a stint of fieldwork in Afghanistan he'd come roaring down the gravel road here in his Saab, came into the kitchen where we were sitting and said several times, with the force that only suddenly obvious insights provide, that we were living in a paradise. That everything here was perfectly paradisiacal. The landscape, the people, even the political system. He saw everything in the light of where he had just been, the war-torn, poor and chaotic country where he had spent the previous weeks.

The neighbour was interested in war too, but in a very different way: while our mutual friend related to it existentially and was concerned with how war affected people, his interest lay in military history, he could expound as knowledgeably about Swedish military campaigns during the seventeenth century as on the German blitzkrieg at the end of the 1930s, spicing it all up with anecdotes and curious facts. Together with his son he often watched documentaries about the Second World War, and in your brother's vocabulary too I had noticed the increasing influence of our neighbour's fascination, for though he was only seven years old and I never talked to him about weapons, torpedoes, submarines, fighter planes, tanks and machine guns kept cropping up in his conversation, often with names of models and other specifics. He always checked to see if the red flag was up or not when we drove past the artillery range; it signalled whether the military were there.

And yet I could hardly imagine a more peaceable and conflict-averse man than this neighbour. He had never been in a war zone, unlike our mutual friend; the closest he'd got was the documentary he was making now, about Ramstein, the gigantic US Army base in Germany. I had seen an outline of the film, and it was strongly anti-militaristic and critical of war.

You had stopped sucking. I took the bottle out of your mouth and set it on the table while you lay there looking up at the ceiling with that gaze that wasn't seeking anything in particular and which seemed entirely open, rather like windows through which light is flowing.

'Daaaaaa,' you said, and your gaze changed, suddenly looking puzzled, as if you were wondering where the sound had come from.

'Well, I guess we should be going,' I said. 'It's a fairly long drive.'

'How long does it take you?'

'A couple of hours,' I said and stood up with you in my arms. He followed us out to the stairs and watched as I strapped you into the seat.

'Well, goodbye then,' I said and slid the side door shut, climbed into the driver's seat and started the car. He remained standing there as I drove through the narrow passage between the houses and out onto the road across the fields, where the sky suddenly seemed higher as the landscape widened out in every direction.

He could have been one of those minor landowners with which Russian literature abounds, I thought. After spending several decades in the bars and restaurants of the capital, gliding in and out of the charged environment surrounding the well known writers and cultural figures of the day, where he had attracted notice as someone who never went home, he had finally, as he approached sixty, moved to the countryside but without finding peace – if that's what he sought – for he still went off to Copenhagen, up to Stockholm or down to Berlin whenever he saw the chance, where he would sit as in the old days, in bars and restaurants, together with his friends, who now, if they hadn't exactly gone downhill, had lost the lustre they once had.

49

I turned left at the end of the gravel road and drove inland towards Ingelstorp for variety's sake. The sun was shining directly through the windscreen, and I lowered the sun visor, opened the lid of the small compartment on top of the dashboard and took out my sunglasses, putting them on as I let go of the wheel with the other hand and changed up, for here the road was as straight as a die.

'What would you like to hear?' I said out loud, mostly so you would understand that you weren't alone in the car, while I opened the glove compartment on the passenger side and rummaged through the pile of CDs. I always chose music without looking, the intention being that it should come as a pleasant surprise, but now the same CDs had been lying there for three years, so the element of surprise had long since vanished.

I slid the CD into the player, still without looking, and turned up the volume.

*London Calling.*

You could do a lot worse.

I slowed down as we approached the crossroads that lay in the middle of the village, with the second-hand bookshop, now open only in summer, on one side of the road and a kind of assembly hall on the other which looked to have been built some time during the 1920s, with the letters FRÖYA set into the brick facade. Back then Norse culture had had a fresh ring to it, full of optimism and future promise, in the years before it was led into the political darkness and lost all its old connotations.

I leaned forward to see if the road up to the church was clear. It was, but instead of turning right, which was the shortest way, I had an impulse to continue straight ahead, and I followed the road between the short row of houses in the village, which I used to think of as flowing like a cape down from the head and shoulders of the church, and out between the tenderly green fields. With the windscreen full of the sun's reflections, which met with resistance in all the scratches I had made the winter I was stupid enough to use CD covers to scrape off the ice, I shot quick glances to the right, where the fields stretched unbroken all the way down to the sea, as I sang along to the music.

*I have no fear, 'cause London is drowning, and I live by the river.*

A bird of prey hovered in the air maybe four metres above the roadway. Its large outstretched wings shone dully in the sunlight and had a woolly look completely at odds with the hard yellow beak and its otherwise streamlined body. There were hundreds of them in the area; whenever I drove to Malmö, I saw one every few kilometres, gliding on the air currents, sitting on poles or crouched over one of the run-over animal carcasses that the motorway was so full of there. Badgers, hedgehogs, rabbits, cats, even the occasional fox.

The children called them *gamar*, which is Swedish for vultures; I didn't know what they were called in Norwegian. Maybe goshawks?

There were goshawks at my maternal grandparents' place, your great-grandparents. Not that I ever saw one, but Grandfather, who was bald except for a white wreath around his head, used to say that the hawk had taken his hair, often illustrating the event with a motion of his hand in which he let his fingers slice down through the air and like a bird with outstretched talons snatch the imaginary hair and fly off with it. For a long time I believed him. I also feared for the hens when they were out in the yard, that the hawk would dive down and snatch one of them.

Grandmother and Grandfather had been dead for more than twenty years, but were still vivid in my memory. To you they would be vague figures in the murk of history; you were born a hundred years after them, and when you entered your twenties, they would represent for you what people born in the 1860s did for me. Which is to say, practically nothing.

The only ones who count are the living.

That's how it's always been, and that's how it will always be. Life clatters within the living, with all their mentalities and psychologies, and when they die and the clatter within them subsides, it continues in their children, and one comes to understand that the clatter was the main thing, the clatter was the point, the clatter was life.

When you reached my present age, I would be over ninety, and if I was still alive then, I would be heading away, taking my leave, in the sense that everything we become attached to, by assigning meaning to it – objects as well as events and people – would be growing more distant, and you, little one, and the life you would then be in the middle of – perhaps with a man, perhaps not, perhaps with children, perhaps not, perhaps with a job that meant a lot to you, perhaps not – would seem to me as a train one sees passing in the forest at dusk, when the air pressure sends the snow swirling and the figures in the lit-up compartments stand out clearly against the black trees and the darkening sky. They would be people like myself, but what they are doing, what they want, what they are thinking and what they feel doesn't matter much, they and the light that surrounds them vanish between the trees almost before they appear, and I gaze up towards the first faint stars beginning to emerge far above me.

Such are the musings of a middle-aged man driving through a sunlit landscape in spring with a small baby in the back seat, I thought. Amid all the clatter of life, where every little thing was significant and a great anxiety about what would happen to us, especially to you children, kept rearing up in me.

'It will turn out fine in the end, don't you think?' I said out loud and changed down as the road twisted in an S-bend between two small round buildings, I had no idea what they were used for and knew nothing about them except that they belonged to the large farm that lay about a kilometre away at the end of a tree-lined avenue.

I had been there several times, since one of your elder sister's classmates lived there. They had a lot of sheep, a lot of horses, the farm buildings were enormous, between them grew huge ancient broadleaved trees. Not many decades ago the place must have employed lots of people, like the farm we had just passed; back then our house had been home to three families who worked there. Mechanisation had made them superfluous, and now whenever I visited, it struck me that there was something odd about the dimensions of the place, that a single man could be in charge of all this, not least the endless fields.

What was odd about it?

It wasn't a reasonable feeling, since it obviously didn't matter how many people did the job, as long as it got done. I had heard once that one could only relate to a certain number of people, that there was a definite limit to humans' ability to maintain stable social relationships, which lay somewhere between a hundred and two hundred people. This limit applied across remarkably varied settings, from military units, which were divided into squads of five soldiers, platoons of twenty-five and companies of a hundred, to the contemporary civilian way of dividing our world, with maybe five very close friends, around twenty-five family members, colleagues or close acquaintances, and from a hundred to a hundred and fifty Facebook friends, marking the outermost limit of one's social circle. In the old days rural communities and villages often numbered about a hundred to a hundred and fifty people, and if one lived in a town one rarely maintained contact with more people than that. And perhaps there existed a similar human limit to everything, including the quantity of land that could be cultivated, which machines had done away with, and which only persisted in this feeling – that it wasn't right, that we were exceeding our limits.

What a conservative thought! But maybe this lay at the origin of my strong, intuitive resistance to mechanisation and the technification of life, the feeling that we were exceeding our boundaries, and that those boundaries were not arbitrary, perhaps not even cultural, but innate to us, just as up and down, left and right were?

I felt strongly that it was wrong to transplant organs, wrong to manipulate genes, wrong to split atoms, and I had always felt that way, but had never been able to present any arguments for my view. It was as if the very process of argumentation, even the intellect itself, belonged to the world of technology and mechanisation and represented everything in us that didn't accept limits, that strove towards what lay beyond us, not just in order to understand it, but to conquer it, so that feelings, which belonged to the body and perceived the world through the body's limitations, were no match for it.

Yes, damn it, there was something fundamentally wrong even about the Internet, I felt.

Well, wasn't there?

'We should have travelled by horse and carriage!' I said out loud, though I suspected you had fallen asleep again, as I slowed down going into the sharp curve and looked at the pond that lay beyond it, glimmering in the sunlight. The pond was man-made, I assumed, and was as big as a small lake; children sometimes sailed on it.

On the other side, at the top of a low hill, the landscape opened out towards the sea in front of us. The view from there was the reason I had taken this roundabout route. Not only was the landscape here beautiful, it also came as a surprise, for since I rarely took this road I perceived the harmony of the surroundings in a new way. The two routes I usually followed defined everything I saw, it was as if the places I passed belonged to the road and were somehow locked to it, isolated from the rest. When I chose one of the other routes, I realised that the landscape was unbroken, that all the farms, all the churches, all the villages lay on the same plain. There was the sea and the beaches it washed against, there was the steep, cliff-like rise which forced the winds upwards, there was the slope down towards the plain, and there was the plain stretching for several kilometres inland to where the forests began.

On the days I had spent alone with you that spring I had often taken you on car rides, it felt so pointless to sit at home with you all those hours while your siblings were at school, and you seemed to enjoy sitting in the back and gazing out, at least you never complained, and I liked to drive, so we would go for a ride around nine, turning down the gravel roads that can still be found here in places, with no other aim than to see something we hadn't seen before. I played music, and I didn't think about anything in particular, for sometimes it's that simple, static thoughts arise in static bodies; if the bodies are set in motion, the thoughts too begin to move.

It wasn't always like that. The previous summer, when your mother had lain in the hospital in Malmö and I would drive in to see her every day, I had had the same thoughts over and over again there in the car, and I had played the same music, Queens of the Stone Age, so loud that it hurt. I wanted it to hurt, for I was hurting inside, and in some way or other the loud, aggressive music helped, as if it provided a counter-pressure.

How strange it had felt to get back home then, after roaring along the motorway with the music blasting for an hour. Turn off the music, reduce the speed to twenty kilometres per hour and roll down the empty warm afternoon quiet of our street, past all the green hedges, the whitewashed houses, turn up the grassy slope, reverse into the driveway next to our red-painted house, switch off the engine, open the door, climb out and feel the warm air pressing against me. The silence reigning there, so specific to sun-filled afternoons in late summer, how the sounds that breach it all seem far away, almost dreamlike, even the sound of the children splashing about in the plastic pool, making a racket, as if the sky is too deep, the world too vast for something as small as a voice to find a foothold in. The rustle in the trees as the offshore breeze comes flowing, the screeching of the hundreds of jackdaws as they settle down in the trees over on the neighbouring property, the faint voices of the neighbours, who have company and are eating outside, the laughter and the clatter of cutlery against dishes.

Those summer weeks, in the sun-warmed and static landscape beneath the deep sky, where everything was blue and green except the saturated gold of the cornfields, were paradisiacal. That's the only word I can find for them, paradisiacal. We ate all our meals outside in the shade of the apple trees, we went swimming at the kilometre-long beaches, we played badminton, barbecued, both your siblings and I had friends visiting; in the evenings, while the sun hung above the roof of the summer house, blazing orange, and the shadows kept lengthening, we sat at the long table outside until faces grew indistinct in the darkness and the children had long since gone to bed.

It was impossible to connect that way of living with the life your mother had at the hospital, and with my trips there, which seemed to belong elsewhere, as if it were a kind of shadow existence, something anaemic and pale, closer to death.

But she was carrying you.

And she must not lose you.

I thought of nothing else.

TWO

More and more often it occurs to me that we live in two realities, one that is physical, material, biological, chemical, the world of objects and bodies, which perhaps we might call reality of the first order, and one that is abstract, immaterial, linguistic and cognitive, the world of relationships and social interactions, which we might call reality of the second order. The first reality is governed by absolute laws which leave no doubt – water freezes at a certain temperature, the apple detaches from the tree when it reaches a certain weight and the gust of wind attains a certain strength, it falls to the ground at a certain velocity, and the impact with the ground causes the flesh of the fruit beneath the skin to bruise in a certain pattern – while the other reality is relative and negotiable. This would be easy to grasp if the two worlds existed side by side, but of course that's not how things are. One world exists within the other, so that an object, for instance a red bucket, is both a red bucket in its own right – conforming to the laws of physics by, for example, melting if it is placed close to a fire, into patterns and forms which are governed by the various factors involved, and which cannot evolve differently – and simultaneously a mental image in the mind of the person contemplating it, where it exists in many different forms: a mass-produced, standardised object standing on the leaf-covered ground next to a pile of soil, recently dug up, in the potato field, hard and non-degradable amid a soft and continually changing nature; a red hollow with a handle for carrying water or gathering up potatoes or apples, standing in a corner of the kitchen; a red glow of something that someone has left behind out in the field, where the fact of having been left behind is really the central aspect, what it says about the people who have left it there, and their careless and slovenly ways; one of the many things that belonged to my parents, which I cannot look at without thinking of my father and of the years we lived together; a red surface melted into a pattern that resembles a human face, from the time my mother set it down a little too close to the fire – yes, over the course of the years that face has come to overshadow the bucket, I see only that face, sticking its tongue out at me across the span of three decades. That a plastic cylinder with a bottom, standing in my mother's broom cupboard, could have so many different identities and be associated with so many feelings . . . What a powerful pull it has, the thought of that bucket standing there in the evening, next to the black, slightly moist soil, on top of the yellow-brown slippery leaves, which the pale green grass shone through in places, at the edge of the forest, that wall of trees which began where the field of potatoes ended, and which now, while my father was digging up the potatoes with a fork, had closed itself up in a dense darkness which seemed to be leaking – at least that's how I imagined it, that darkness was seeping from between the trees and out across the field, where the air that only half an hour earlier had been limpid became more and more grey, and the silence

too kept growing – great is the silence of the forest at night –
so that the only sounds, besides the nearly inaudible tremor
that passed through the trees when a breath of wind
brushed through them, were the sounds of the fork being
thrust into the ground, tinkling faintly as the hard metal slid
through the loose soil, the boot stamping on it, the rustling
as my father tossed the earth aside, his breathing. The
bucket standing there, glowing in the gathering murk,
which had held all kinds of things – live crabs, still wet and
salty from the sea, dead fish, slimy and soft, until a reflex
convulsed their muscles and their tails thrashed once or
twice in that peculiar movement which is an expression of
neither life nor death, but something in between, akin to the
movements of wind and water, apples, pears, plums, blue-
berries, raspberries, blackberries, sloes, rubbish, clean and
dirty water, dry and wet cloths, bottles of detergent . . .

My identity, the person I am to myself, is woven into the
world of things in such a way that it is impossible to say where
one ends and the other begins, while my body is, in a sense,
itself an object, as finite as other objects, just as limited but
also just as open, since water runs not only down through the
ground but also down through the gullet, and the air which
fills up every hollow also fills the lungs, to say nothing of all
the plants and animals we ingest and then expel again when
we've absorbed everything that is of use to us – and one day
the body will enter the world of things completely, become an
object among other objects, like a leaf, a log, a hillock, and go
on existing as elements of a mute reality.

You too, my child, are a thing, a soft little four-limbed
creature, biologically determined, with a heart that will beat
a certain number of times.

When did your life begin?

It was when two cells from two different bodies fused into one and the new cell began to divide. It happened at a particular moment in a particular place in the world. But as if stretched over this mute and self-sufficient biology another narrative extends, the social one, in which nothing has either beginning or end, and the start of your story, what would become your life, might as well have been when your mother was born, or the time we saw each other for the first time, one sunny afternoon on an inland island in Sweden in the summer of 1999, or the time we first began to speak about the possibility of having another child.

That happened in May 2013, when your mother and I travelled to Sydney in Australia, where I was taking part in a literary festival. The hotel as well as the venues for the festival events lay by the water, in buildings I was fairly certain had once been old warehouses. My body was tuned to the daily rhythm of life at home, and I felt as if a battle was being fought inside it, between my senses, for whom it was undoubtedly night, with dense, rain-filled darkness outside the windows and silence reigning in every room and corridor, and the deeper structures of the brain, for whom it was day, and which therefore prevented me from sleeping: I lay wide awake in bed, gazing up at the ceiling, or sat in the chair in front of the sliding glass door looking out at the terrace and the quayside walkway beyond it, lit by street lamps, and the black, lifeless water extending to the next pier maybe fifty metres further on. The rain and the water and the light glistening upon the buildings reminded me of Bergen, and even though I knew I was in Australia, on the other side of the globe, in Sydney, it was as if the sensation of being in

Bergen trumped reason, so that I was actually there. That my body and my senses were undermining each other in this way, vacillating between day and night, spring and autumn, Bergen and Sydney, past and present, gave reality an evasive air, it was almost as if I was sleepwalking. The sensation was even stronger during the daytime, when not even the hours of sunlight, during which every surface was illuminated and every colour stood out sharply, could overwhelm the feeling I had that it was actually night, that it was actually dark. I sensed the darkness within the light, I sensed the night within the day, and the impulse to sleep was so powerful that it no longer resembled fatigue, which can be shaken off and resisted, but appeared as a thing apart, a force building within me, a bow that in the next instant, if I lay down, would shoot me like an arrow into sleep.

Once when I was a child, I entered the living room of the house where I grew up, the television set was turned on, no one else was there, and I glanced at the screen, where a headless person was walking up a staircase. It must have been an afternoon film, for I remember that the sun was shining outside, on a wet autumnal landscape, and it must have been a Sunday, since I was at home. I can't have been very old, maybe seven or eight, and it frightened me more than anything I had ever experienced. That it happened in broad daylight made it that much worse, it was as if there were no safe places left. If you are afraid of the dark, you seek the light. But what do you do when even the light is filled with terrors?

I wasn't afraid in Sydney, but I saw the same thing I had seen as a child, the darkness within the light, the night within the day. What I saw, and what I had once been afraid of but no longer was, was the shadow of the unknown. That all people, all faces, all voices belonged to strangers. That even Mum and Dad were strangers. This is the fear awakened by every horror movie, every ghost story, every tale about vampires, zombies, revenants and doppelgängers, but when it is linked to darkness, somehow isolated from the rest of life, it is titillating, for although the fear arises because the shadow of the unknown is a reality, it is limited, day will come, in the light of which the unknown will dissolve and the familiar return.

The person with no attachments is an anomaly, since almost everything we do is about forming attachments to others and about establishing relationships that feel permanent, that we can trust will last. So strong is this inclination that the attachment doesn't have to be to people we know, friends or family, to become significant; it can be to a voice on the radio, a face on television, a sales assistant at the supermarket, a first-person narrator in a book. The only time I've been physically alone over a longer period, when I spent a few months on a small island to write, and the absence of other people felt like a hard-to-define yet powerful deficiency, almost physical, akin to other states of deficiency such as that of salt or sunlight, I grew attached to certain voices on the radio, I turned it on whenever their programmes were about to air, there was pleasure associated with listening to them just as meeting a friend can be associated with pleasure. The same was true of a diary I was reading at the time. It comforted me, although for many this will seem a meagre comfort, since these odd friendships weren't mutual, neither the voice on the radio nor the author of the book knew who I was, they naturally never felt any connection to me, and I suppose even I felt that the comfort they offered was scant, just as one tends to think of the comfort lonely old people find in television as being meagre and actually rather awful, for they are people made of flesh and blood, and the faces on TV, which they perhaps smile at occasionally, are merely pixels luring them into an artificial closeness, something deeply inauthentic, a reality they only pretend to believe in.

But imagine then, my little one, a state of being truly lonely, in which you don't know anyone, don't talk to anyone, and where nobody sees you, they merely look away. Such absolute loneliness would be impossible to live in, for why would one go on living at all? Everything within us is directed towards others. Language is directed towards others, and with it our thoughts, and with them, as the innermost existential truth, also the self. As long as the self exists in a space where there are others, even if only in the form of a voice on the radio, a face on TV, a narrator in a book, there is meaning, it can lead a meaningful life. But because the self is structured as an address to someone else, if it is deprived of others it can only be maintained by the will, and since the will of the self is merely the will for there to be others, sooner or later, if not even the slightest hope remains, the self will be extinguished.

If the person without attachments is an anomaly, then so is suicide. There are as many reasons for suicide as there are people who commit suicide, but common to them all is that in one way or another they have become unattached, something other than attachment has gained the upper hand within them, making them unable to receive what the self needs to live. This impossibility of attachment is often temporary, for the darkness within, this stiffening of the soul which nothing external can penetrate or move, which we call clinical depression, is a state, acute but not unchangeable: even in the dark night of the soul there comes a dawn. In some way or other we all know this, all except the suicide, for whom the darkness and the pain are so great that not even the certainty that it will get better can make it bearable. For whom the darkness and pain are so great that not even the sight of one's own children is enough to overcome the longing for the final darkness, the death of the self.

Suicide can also be a way to create meaning. It is an act, and acts always mean something, not only through their consequences, but also in their intentions. A girl I once knew worked at an institution one summer, she told me how the director's son had shot himself in the head with a shotgun on the lawn outside his father's office. A young man on the periphery of my circle of acquaintances hanged himself beneath the staircase of his mother's house on her birthday. He had a small child. Both wanted to point to something, look here, they said through their act, look what you have done to me. Someone else I knew dressed in a black suit, a white shirt and a tie and hanged himself in his apartment; he had two children. All of his adult life he had romanticised death, idolised it. Maybe it was a way to make the pain bearable, turning death into something desirable?

Both these acts, to point out, aggressively and irrevocably, the guilt of another for one's pain, and to romanticise death, are infantile and familiar to all of us: who as a child hasn't fantasised about the grief others will feel as they follow our coffin to the grave, where they finally realise the injustice that has been done to us? Only there, we seem to think, only

68

in death will our true worth become visible to others, as suddenly as a light switched on in a dark room.

What is this if not a wish for attachment? Which at one and the same time is granted and extinguished, that impossible gesture of which Orpheus' gaze is an eternal image. It is childish, yet it doesn't belong to childhood, for suicide is alien to childhood. Youth, with its tempestuous moods, its impulsivity and lack of understanding of the consequences, can be a dangerous age; the only time I actually considered taking my own life, instead of just flirting with the possibility the better to appreciate the value and richness of life, which along with guilt immediately wells up at the thought that I could, if I wanted to, simply turn the wheel and drive straight into the approaching lorry, but actually considered it, I was eighteen years old, on my way home from a party one early summer morning, through the industrial landscape on the outskirts of Kristiansand, drunk and unable to parry the blow of the experience that had made me leave the party without telling anyone. It was a small matter, everyone had laughed at me, even those I trusted most and felt closest to, and the thought that no one liked me and that I was worthless, which was usually only one thought among many, had in my intoxication gained enormous sway over me. I climbed up a mountain, intending to throw myself off it, and as I stood there, the thought that it was actually possible, that in the next instant my life could be over, rose within me like a wave of exultation. I remember my despair, and I remember the exultation, but I don't remember what stopped me, why half an hour later I climbed down again and continued on my way home. But it was probably my mum, imagining her grief. And perhaps that image was the real reason I went up there, perhaps that's what I was seeking, the idea that someone loves me, someone needs me?

I notice that I don't really like talking about it, for my suffering was so minor and nothing really happened, but what I am getting at, my child, is that when you are in your teens, all it takes is a minor dislocation to find yourself in a similar situation, and if you are just a little more drunk or a little more despairing, you might suddenly do what would normally be unthinkable. Once when I was on a mountain trip in northern Norway, the guide told us that there had been a wave of suicides among local youths. Once the first youth had done it, it became a possibility, and it took less for the next person to follow suit, and then the next and the next person after that again.

My father, your grandfather, occasionally talked about suicide as a phenomenon. He was interested in the Norwegian author Jens Bjørneboe, both in his 1955 novel *Jonas* attacking the public school system – maybe because my father was himself a teacher; he sometimes borrowed the novel's pejorative term salamanders to criticise fellow teachers – and in Bjørneboe's suicide, the purely practical side of it, how he did it. He also talked about his belief that the number of actual suicides was probably higher than officially reported, and that many head-on collisions, for instance, were really hidden suicides. Back then I didn't realise that there is always a reason why someone talks about one subject rather than another, I just listened to what he said, probably also commented on it, as one issue among others, without understanding that it meant something, that it said something about what was stirring within him. He died not many years later as a result of careless heavy drinking, which it is hard not to view as a slow suicide. He wanted to die, and he died.

Why did he want to die?

He was a person without attachments. He wrote about it once in his diary, that he had always been a lonely person.

There was no shortage of people or love around him, the deficiency was within himself, he was unable to receive, unable to form attachments.

You see, the beauty of this world means nothing if you stand alone in it.

If one is approaching the age of fifty and begins to list all the people one has met or heard of who have come to a bad end, it seems staggering, as if life is a hard and joyless burden which only a few manage to get through without being pushed down into the darkness. But that's not how it is, because this roll of individuals doesn't take time into consideration, that vast sea of days and nights which waters down every event, and which is constantly expanding, growing larger. Any cataloguing of cases distorts reality, and what we think of as our lives, in which the decisive moments are crowded close together, is to reality as a map is to the terrain, or the stars to the starry sky: viewed from here, the distance between them appears insignificant, from here one would think the stars in the universe are as closely packed as a shoal of herring, but if one were to travel out to them, one would realise that the truth about the universe is the space in between.

That is why a work like Jens Bjørneboe's trilogy The History of Bestiality, that catalogue of infamies, atrocities and abuses, is true sentence for sentence, but as a whole it is a deception. Certainly evil exists, but it is insignificant in relation to non-evil. Certainly darkness exists, but merely as pinpricks in the light. Certainly life is painful, but the pain is merely a kind of invisible channel that we follow through what is otherwise neutral or good, and which we sooner or later emerge from.

That's how it was for your mother and me when we went to Sydney, we had emerged from something so trying that we had just barely managed to parry it. It had culminated in a severe depression, with your mother lying motionless in bed, unable to perform even the least demanding of actions, such as listening to the radio or reading, much less get dressed, get up and face the day. The times I helped her do that and we took a little walk in the park, slowly like an elderly married couple, she would sit down on a bench and cry ceaselessly in a grief that must have been bottomless. Your grandmother, my mother, came down to help us, and your mother's mother came; once when I was going to pick up the children and your mother's mother was going out on an errand, we suddenly looked at each other outside the front door, and she turned around without a word and ran back: we both understood at the same instant that your mother couldn't be left alone in that darkness, that in the darkness she was in she might be driven to do something to make it stop so that the pain would cease.

After darkness came light, but that too was overwhelming and uncontrollable, and she was hospitalised. When that had passed, towards the end of the summer, and she came back home, we bought the house where we are living now, it was supposed to be a summer house. We came out here every Friday and drove back every Sunday evening. Life stabilised, even though these events stayed alive within her, like a kind of reverberation, for the oscillations between high and low were still noticeable even if no longer unmanageable, and they gradually became smaller and smaller. We moved into the house and began living here. Your sisters started school here, your brother went to kindergarten. For the first time since we had become a family we had money, we bought our first car, we went for trips around the area, we went on holidays, and I began to work in the garden, which my father had always done, and which I could never have imagined myself doing. After two years here, in the first house that had felt like a home to me since the one I grew up in, your mother began talking about having another child. She wasn't serious about it, I don't think, it was more like she was expressing a longing, and I said no, no way, three is more than enough. But the thought had been planted, and a child for me symbolised a turning point, a new beginning, at the same time as it entailed a commitment of a kind that I probably knew I needed, deep inside, at the bottom of myself, where I knew that it made me a better person. I liked myself when I was with the children, that was one of the great joys they gave me, and I liked no one as much as I liked them. A new child would create more love, and it would make it impossible for me ever to choose another life than with my family.

When we went to Sydney, I took with me *Scenes From a Marriage*, Ingmar Bergman's 1970s film, since later that summer I was supposed to participate in Bergman Week on the isle of Fårö, and the film is so long that I hadn't had time to watch it at home. So there we sat, your mother and I, ten years into our relationship, on a plane headed for Australia, watching an almost-documentary movie about the dissolution of another Swedish–Norwegian relationship forty years before. We joked about it, how it must look from the outside, but we also relished it, it was the kind of thing we'd done at the beginning of our relationship, watched movies together, discussed them, not least Bergman's films, which were a part of her childhood and youth, and which had overwhelmed me in my late twenties. I was struck by the film's authenticity, its candour and intensity, and I thought that must be why it didn't seem dated in the way other movies from the 1970s did, or for that matter the rest of Bergman's films – they belonged within the film world, and while they were still watchable because that world was in a sense complete and self-enclosed, similar to how fairy tales were readable although the world they dealt with had few points of contact with ours, this film was open to reality in an altogether different way. Presumably, that was why the absence of children was so striking. I could relate to everything else, the hatred, the frustration, the malice, the togetherness and the love, which seemed to flow in waves between the two main characters without ever settling, and precisely because I identified with them, I found it striking that their children had no part in the rupture or the feelings it occasioned in them. Was it Bergman or was it the age?

It must be the age. I myself had grown up during the 1970s, and I remembered how separate the adult world had been. It was as if it played out on a plateau, while the children lived their lives in the valley beneath, where we were allowed to do as we pleased. At times we could see the adults standing up there looking down at us, but they hardly ever climbed down into the valley, nor were we allowed up onto the plateau very often. Our teachers stood up there, parents stood up there, the sales assistants in the shops, the swimming pool attendants, coaches and scoutmasters stood up there. Events in the adult world, such as a divorce, existed as rumours down below, but were impossible to control, so that they often became distorted and cemented in peculiar varieties of reality.

This sounds like something from another age. And so it is. *Scenes From a Marriage* is to your birth year what a film from 1928 is to mine.

Maybe some day you will see the movie. And if you do, maybe you will see something entirely different which I am blind to?

We had a stopover in Singapore, where the humidity felt like a wall when we went out onto a terrace in the middle of the night to have a smoke, while in Sydney a few hours later the weather was cool, the air cold and clear, full of trickling raindrops. As we drove towards the city on the broad jet-black tarmac road, I talked to the driver who had come to pick us up about Australian bands. 'The Church,' I said. 'Oh, the Church!' he said as the lights we were passing beneath seemed to pulse through the car. 'The Hoodoo Gurus,' I said. 'Oh yeah,' he said. 'But The Go-Betweens were the best, weren't they?' I said. 'You might be right,' he said. 'Yes, you might be right. Where are you guys from?' 'Norway,' I said and looked at your mother sitting next to me. 'Sweden,' she said. 'We live in Sweden.' 'In Sweden?' he said. 'There are riots in Sweden now.' 'Really?' I said. 'Riots in Sweden?' 'Yes, as we are talking. It's in the news.'

'Can that be right?' I said, looking at her.

'I have no idea,' she said. 'Sounds strange.'

We drove into the city, which looked quite different to how I had imagined, I had had a vague image of broad sun-filled streets issuing onto beaches, while what we were driving through was dense, dark, rainy, and even though I saw a flash of the famous opera house on the other side of the bay, fully lit, the next instant I was reminded of Bergen, when the road circled a low mountain and came out into a port area, where shortly after the car stopped and we got out.

We checked in and got unpacked, I had a smoke standing on the balcony and looking out over the black surface of the water glistening with lights, from which piers rose further on, black like the water. The riots in Sweden, which had sounded apocalyptic in the car, turned out to be a couple of cars that had been set on fire in a suburb outside Stockholm. It looked dramatic on TV, but probably wasn't in reality.

Your mother had lain down on the bed inside, I saw, flicking the cigarette out onto the concrete deck and opening the sliding door.

'Are you tired?' I said.

'Nothing to worry about,' she said. 'Are you?'

I shook my head.

'Should we go out and get some food?'

'Yes.'

We followed the road the car had taken, around an embankment beneath a glittering bridge that reared up in the rain, and entered an area with low buildings and several pubs and restaurants. Your mother was quiet, as if imbued with the darkness. I thought that state was the one closest to her nature, that she was closest to being herself when she was like this, and in any case closest to her surroundings.

Now we could talk to each other. Not that we talked about

anything important. It was the way it happened that was important. It was grounded in a reality that we shared, and what we said mattered. It was binding.

That's how things had been between us when we became a couple ten years ago, and around the time your siblings were born. And that's how it was now. During these days we were closer to each other than we had been for several years, not just because she was fully present, but also because I had turned towards her again, I wasn't shutting her out, as I had done for so long.

We talked about the children, your three siblings, whom we had never been away from together for that length of time. We took joy in talking about them, who they were, what they were up to, what might have happened to them in the course of their day. Two Scandinavians at a table in an Italian restaurant one rainy spring evening in Sydney, long silences between them, as one can so often observe between married couples in restaurants but never considers a possibility in one's own life.

But it was nice. And when we came home a week later, the children were waiting for us in the hall, excited and happy. They got presents, which the youngest unwrapped at breakneck speed, with the greed of a six-year-old, the older two proceeding at a more dignified pace, and they were full of questions about what we had seen and done. Australia was a country they felt strongly about, since they had seen it in so many TV series, and our being there was the next best thing to being there themselves. We told them we had seen the opera house, that it was autumn there and not very warm, that it really looked rather like it did here, and that one evening we had had dinner in a restaurant on the top of a cliff above the ocean, which struck the land beneath us in huge waves as we ate.

'Were there sharks there?'

'Did you see kangaroos?'

'Did the children wear school uniforms?'

They hung around us, wouldn't let go, told us about everything that had happened while we were away.

That your mother was pregnant with you that evening, nobody knew.

Some weeks later, a little into the school holiday, we went to Fårö, where we were given rooms in Ingmar Bergman's guesthouse, a few hundred metres from where he himself had lived during the last forty years of his long life. We left home at noon, driving along the coast north to Oskarshamn, where the ferry to Gotland left. Our car, a Multivan, had a large space in the back where the seats faced each other with a table between them, and while your siblings would some-times protest before we left on a longer journey, there was a part of them that liked it, it seemed, once they had accepted the basic premise of sitting still in a car seat for hours on end, interrupted by stops at petrol stations and roadside cafés. They quickly entered a kind of comatose state, looking apathetically out the window at the landscape whizzing by, then suddenly livening up at irregular intervals, which might end in a laughing fit or a quarrel or fade away into a new silence.

I had only taken this route a couple of times before, and it felt as if I was driving through the outer reaches of my memory, where I never knew what the next stretch would look like but still recognised it as soon as it appeared. It was a little like reading a novel again, where you might feel the approach of something familiar but, however hard you might try, be wholly unable to remember it before it happens, and the event or the description gains that special fullness which arises when the seemingly new, happening as if for the first time, encounters the memory of how it was the last time, and the space between your inner version of reality and external reality for a moment stands open, until the external, which has a much more powerful presence, obliterates the internal reality, and the world becomes one again.

The sun was low in the sky as we left the main road and drove towards Oskarshamn, where the ferry was waiting at the dock, and it was dark as we drove down the ramp on the other side, in the middle of the long line of cars, which stayed close together during the first hundred-metre stretch in the port area but then spread out more and more as the road branched, then branched again and again, until we were the only ones left, as we sped north through the stunted forest characteristic of Gotland, full of bogs, groves, glades, fields, lying there peacefully in the stillness of the night. The plains were faintly visible against the black trees, a dense mass in the darkness, here and there mist lingered over them, while the light of the headlamps, which seemed so brutal amid all the subtle gradations of darkness, flooded the road ahead and flashed back from the lines on the road and reflector posts as we put kilometre after kilometre behind us and approached the northern end of the island, where another ferry would take us to Fårö.

One previous summer we had spent a holiday on Gotland, when we had one child and your mother was six months gone with the second. We lived in Stockholm then and had talked about moving to Gotland, I remember. I must have been the one who wanted it most, I had always felt drawn to remote areas, but your mother was open to the idea too, even though her whole life was in Stockholm and she had never lived anywhere else. We wanted to start again, and neither of us had a realistic outlook on life; a beautiful landscape or a romantic notion was enough to arouse a longing in us that was stronger than any practical objections. That was also why we were expecting another child back then. To have hope, to go after our dreams and then deal with things as they came up, that was our strategy.

One afternoon I was doing the dishes while your mother was asleep upstairs. I looked out the window above the kitchen counter, at the light rain falling steadily outside, where the grey light made the green glow with that peculiar intensity typical of rainy Nordic summers, which I liked so well, not least because it reminded me of all the summers I had spent in western Norway, where it rained all the time and the landscape possessed a kind of cold lushness, green as a jungle but without the jungle's steaming luxuriance, more like a sober wildness, a cool ecstasy.

Trout, foaming waterfalls, shimmering grass along the hillsides, clouds dragging their underbellies over the water. Grey and green, green and grey. My hands in the lukewarm dishwater, covered in a light mesh of soap bubbles every time I lifted them to place a glass or a plate on the grey metal rack next to the sink. The sudden thought of your sister, whom I hadn't seen for a few minutes. The panic that rose in me, and which I kept in check by doing everything slowly. I put down the dish brush on the counter, bright artificial

yellow with nearly unused white bristles, and dried my wrin-
kled fingers on my shorts as I walked out into the garden
calling her name. First I looked across the lawn, then towards
the road and the forest beyond. She couldn't have gone into
the woods, could she? I didn't think so, based on the intuition
all parents have in relation to their children, that one knows
roughly what they might and might not get themselves into,
and I entered the house again and glanced into the living
room, but she wasn't there either. Then I heard steps on the
ceiling above me. She had gone up into the attic. There were
no stairs, just a ladder. Had she climbed up the ladder? She
could get herself killed! She could barely walk!

I hurried upstairs, and she turned to face me, with her
nappy drooping duck-like from her bottom, and smiled. You
little loon, I said and lifted her up, carried her downstairs.
What did you go up there for? Don't you know that the stairs
are dangerous? No, she said without understanding what
my words meant, and looked expectantly at me.

All parents have experienced these things, when something could go wrong but doesn't. All it takes is a slight
change of circumstances, a sound which makes her turn
round, lose her balance and fall head first onto the cement
floor, but the sound doesn't come, she doesn't lose her balance, it turns out fine, almost always. Even a fairly small
child is competent in its own way, and it takes a lot for something to go really wrong. But it happens, to be alive is also to
be always in the proximity of death.

In the afternoons I went running on the forest roads, and if
I took pleasure in the beauty of the green glow of the forest
and meadows against the grey rain-filled sky, that was

nothing to what I felt the first time I saw the *rauks* standing in between the trees, those characteristic rock formations left behind along the beaches of Gotland after the sea had weathered away the softer types of rock from the geological strata they were once a part of, and which look man-made, like statues or monuments, at the same time that they seem twisted, distorted by something resembling rage against the immobility to which everything made of stone is condemned. I found them beautiful in themselves, but here, rearing up from the mossy forest floor in between the tree trunks, there was something unworldly about them, something deeply foreign and yet strangely full of promise: when I stopped in front of them, there were tears in my eyes.

The soughing of the waves striking the deserted pebble beach just below, the vast silence of the sky, the reddish trunks of the pines, the dry green of their sprigs, so pale against the juicy greedy green of the moss, the totem-like rocks that were as tall as people, as if left behind there by another age, itself long past.

That must have been why there were tears in my eyes, I have since thought, because of the rift in time they created, that they were here, and that here had always existed.

I ran on, I ran home, I ran to your mother with her big belly and to your sister with her little body, I ran towards my family, I ran towards everything I had.

Eight years later, your two sisters and their little brother were sitting sleepily in the back seat as we approached the ferry landing at the north end of the same island. Your mother, who was sitting next to me, was quiet; I thought she had begun the strange withdrawal that I recognised from her previous pregnancies, a state which wasn't exactly introverted, for she was fully present in everything she did, it was more as if whatever went on outside her wasn't as important, that the truly important thing, what carried weight, happened inside her.

That I was constantly noting her mood, that I interpreted everything she said and did as a part of a larger pattern, was not unlike what I had done with my father when I was growing up. Then as now, I was engaged in a kind of meteorology of the mind, because my own existence in a sense depended on it.

Now things were fine.

We drove through a small settlement and saw the ferry shining on the water below. Except for one car parked on the other side of the deck, near the sea gate at the prow, the ferry was empty. No sooner had I driven on board and parked behind the other car than the ferry set itself in motion. We went out onto the deck, which was flooded with industrial-strength light, and stood at the railing gazing out into the soft summer darkness, where the water in the sound and the sky were a tiny shade lighter than the land of the two islands, which lay like black silhouettes on either side.

'Are we there soon?' your elder sister said.

'Yes,' I said. 'I'm going to call them and tell them we're here.'

I walked a little away from the others, lit a cigarette and got out the piece of paper the organisers had sent me, giving directions as well as a phone number I was supposed to call when we were nearly there, so they could give us the keys. I dialled the number while I looked over towards the others, three children standing close beside their mother and gazing out across a silent sound at night, the mother lifting the smallest child up so that he too could see. The thought that you were there too, in the tiny, fragile beginnings of your life. A woman answered my call, I told her we were on the ferry, she explained which road to take, saying that it could be a little difficult to find and I should feel free to call again if we got lost. We had been to Fårö too, that summer eight years ago, and I remembered that we had been half expecting to recognise Ingmar Bergman's house, which we knew from countless films and photographs but which we also knew lay in an isolated spot, and about which the local inhabitants were known never to answer any questions. Bergman himself was still alive at the time, though I had no wish to meet him, I never have when it comes to artists or writers, since the appeal in their works is always so much more direct and personal than in reality and feels much closer there than it can ever be face to face. What is literature an expression of, if not an otherwise inaccessible and in reality non-existent closeness? If we still kept a lookout for the long, low and brown-stained wooden house that lay above one of the island's many pebble beaches right at the edge of the forest, it was because of the attraction it held as a landmark, which makes one seek out sights one has heard of when arriving in a new place. And perhaps also because Bergman was such a mythic figure that it seemed almost impossible that he should actually exist and be physically present at a particular place at a particular time. That his work over time had grown so extensive that he himself had disappeared into it and become a fictional character.

Oh, so *this* is where we were, I thought when a couple of kilometres from the ferry landing we turned right and not long after that turned left into a gravel road full of holes, which first ran past a couple of small open fields and then disappeared into the darkness of the pine forest.

The road was narrow and winding, and the cone of light from the headlamps shone just as often in between the ghostly tree trunks as down the road ahead. We drove past a house on the left, surrounded by a tall wire fence – that must be Bergman's home – and a few hundred metres after that the road ended at two houses with a little gravel yard in front.

'Are we there?' one of your sisters said.

'We're here!' I said and turned off the ignition, pulled on the handbrake.

'Finally!' the other one said.

'I need to go to the bathroom really badly,' your brother said.

As we climbed out of the car and I opened the luggage compartment to take out the suitcases and backpacks and the shopping bags full of food, the door of one of the houses opened, it was the woman I had spoken with on the phone. She bade us welcome and went through the practicalities while your brother stood staring into the forest with a wild look in his eyes, then ran into the house when we finally got the key and she left us, while I carried in the luggage and the girls immediately began to quarrel about who would sleep where in the rooms upstairs.

Since I was supposed to speak about Bergman while we were there, I had reread two of his novels, *The Best Intentions* and *Private Confessions*. I had completely forgotten how important they had been to me when I read them for the first time, and how greatly they had influenced my first novel. Bergman's novels are about his parents, called Anna and

Henrik in his books. The first one tells the story of how they met and became a couple, the second deals with an episode a few years later when Anna has an affair with a divinity student and chooses to confess. The portrayal of the father in particular made an impression on me, how he was an expression of what I privately called 'infantile authority', which I thought was also characteristic of my own father, to such an extent that it influenced the depiction of the father in my own book, where the middle part tells the story of how the parents of the main character, whom I named Henrik, met each other. I still can't read that part, for although it represents a period in the lives of my father and mother in a way that in one sense is accurate, and is meaningful also in other ways, it rings false. I hadn't experienced what I was writing about, and here I am not thinking of the actual events, but what they represented. It didn't resonate within me, it wasn't rooted in me, and that made it fundamentally untrue, even though superficially it was correct. This is ironic, since what concerned me most while I was reading these books was precisely the question of truth. 'No one can commit violence against the Truth without going wrong. Without doing harm,' says Jacob, the old parish priest from whom Anna had received confirmation in *Private Confessions*, after Anna has confessed. But the truth itself entails violence, and it is between these two opposing insights that the novel plays itself out.

Liv Ullmann made the screen version of *Private Confessions*, and the film nearly hypnotised me when I saw it at the age of twenty-seven. I can't have understood very much of it, at least not in the way I understand it now. But it had great emotional force, and I was defenceless against it. At the time

I thought that what the film showed was 'the naked life'. Therefore it didn't matter that the experiences it dealt with, infidelity in marriage and the turmoil it occasioned, were not ones that I myself had had, not even remotely. For the emotions they unleashed didn't belong to the act of infidelity, or so I thought, but to the naked life. Life as it appears when the outward forms break down, or when one is absolutely true to oneself, which are perhaps one and the same thing.

I had long considered that knowledge was academic knowledge, that experience was academic experience, and that this was what a writer, a film director or an artist should convey. That a novel, a film or a work of art contained an insight, and that reading meant wresting this insight from the work. At the time when I first saw Liv Ullmann's movie and read Ingmar Bergman's books, I began to think that academic knowledge, academic experience, intellectual insights were nothing but a form of protection against the naked life. And that most books, films and works of art were too.

This ran counter to everything I had learned, it was downright anti-intellectual, but at the same time it was consistent with something I had always known, and beginning in my late teens had always resisted, namely the superiority of ingenuousness. Bergman was never an ingenuous director, quite the opposite, and unlike the movie, his novel *Private Confessions* is not ingenuous either. It is concerned with the consequences of truth, with the price of freedom, and it plays this out in the simplest and most psychologically precise way. Anna's mother warns her against Henrik, she understands that he is bad for her, that he is a needy person who will demand everything of her, and that in order to give it to him she will be forced to renounce her own life, her own self. But she is young, and she is in love, and she follows her heart. When, several years later, she encounters Jacob the priest in the churchyard in Uppsala, she is leading a double life, she is in love with Thomas the student and sees him secretly while living with Henrik and the children she has with him. This time she knows what she is doing, she has weighed everything up and her actions are deliberate. That her love for Thomas is also destructive, and that these two forces, infatuation and destruction, in the novel are associated with freedom, make Anna the sister of another adulterous woman in literature, I am thinking of Tolstoy's Anna Karenina, who finally sees suicide as the only solution and throws herself in front of a train. The men they fall in love with also have certain traits in common, both are younger than them, both are considerably more immature, and both are seen clearly, with all their faults, and yet they are loved.

What kind of love is this?

In Tolstoy's manifold works there is another character who possesses the same gaze and who expresses the same kind of love, I am thinking of Princess Maria in *War and Peace*, who towards the end marries Nikolai Rostov, and who is in a sense far superior to him. She sees him with all his failings and shortcomings, his immaturity and his vanity, while he sees nearly nothing of her, yet she loves him. The gaze with which she regards him resembles that of parents looking at their children – at least I see my children in that way, I invariably know more about them than they know themselves, why they do what they do, say what they say, I see all their faults and failings, while they are aware neither of these nor my gaze upon them, which is filled with an unconditional love that almost grows more intense the weaker they appear. This isn't really so strange when one stops to consider it, for Ingmar Bergman was writing about his mother when he wrote about Anna, and Leo Tolstoy was writing about his mother when he wrote about Maria; she shares all her traits and her entire life story, as is shown by Henri Troyat's biography of him.

If I were to write about my mother's love for my father, that is how I too would describe it. That is the only way I can understand what she once told me, that she loved him. As for me, I am unable to love in that way. But for a long time that is how I wanted to be loved.

We lived in this Bergmanesque summer house on Fårö for five days, long enough to fall into a certain rhythm: in the mornings I drove to the grocery shop to buy breakfast, before noon we drove to one of the beaches on the north-eastern side of the island to swim, eating dinner at an outdoor restaurant there, and in the evenings, after the children had gone to bed, we watched Bergman films, since I was terrified of coming unprepared to the event I was to participate in.

One evening your sisters stayed up sitting on the sofa with us, we saw *The Seventh Seal*, and they were transfixed. In particular, the witch who was bound to a wall interested them, what wrong she had done, they kept referring to that scene for several months afterwards. I think what fascinated them was firstly that the notion of witches wasn't just something that belonged to the world of fairy tales, it also existed in historical reality, that came as a small shock to them, and secondly that in this reality it wasn't actually true, but people believed it to be true, so that certain women were treated as witches anyway. I told them about the witch trials and the ordeal by water, that they were tied up and thrown into water. If they floated, I said, they were witches and were burned, if they sank they weren't witches and were allowed a Christian burial. But they died either way! they said. That's so unfair! They weren't witches! No, they weren't, I said. But that was a long time ago. The world was different then. To us it seems almost like a fairy tale. And what you saw was a movie. The woman who was bound to the wall was an actress.

I in turn was fascinated by their fascination, for though they lived in the same house, walked around in the same world as us, they related to it in different ways, in which little of what we thought about and experienced existed. We hardly ever watched the news on TV, so that visual explosion and concentration of violence and accidents, problems and concerns was something that merely existed in the background, as a vague backdrop which might suddenly become relevant, as when one day the elder one said she thought Putin was evil or that the Sweden Democrats were an evil party, or when out of the blue her sister asked, as I was reversing the car to park outside the house, why the Nazis had killed the Jews. In a strange way, I enjoyed witnessing this fracturing of their safe, harmless reality, for it was as much a case of them taking steps up into the adult world as of the world filtering down to them, and I thought of it as a conquest, that they would take their places in it. That the greed for understanding was just as important as feeling safe. Other parts of the adult world – what existed between your mother and me and between us and our relatives and friends – they accepted unquestioningly, since in a sense these formed the condition of their lives, but I noticed how our sympathies and antipathies were transmitted to them, that our conflicts, even if they were unexpressed, caused them to choose sides in so many small ways, as if driven by an unconscious need to establish a balance.

They were like water, they flowed in where there was room and there were openings, turned aside where there were none.

During those days on Fårö your mother was withdrawn, she didn't say much, but often brightened up when we were on the beach, as if the vast pale blue sky and the blazing light also shone into her dark thoughts. I didn't mind her silence, for these were good days, and there was so much in them that I enjoyed. Not in an intense or ecstatic way, it was more that they were filled with little puffs of satisfaction. The feeling of the warm car seat against my thighs when I sat down in it wearing shorts. The joy of being a functioning family, when I had loaded the bags full of beach things into the car and everyone had climbed in, and I started the car and drove along the narrow shady gravel road. The buzzing of insects in the air above the flowers when I sat on the bench in the shade by the wall, smoking, or when all of us sat around the table outside in the morning, eating breakfast in the garden, where it was already warm. The grass-covered field that served as a car park at the beach, which reminded me of the car park where my grandparents would leave their car before we took the boat out to their cabin when I was small. The black tyres, the green grass, the shadows cast by the birches we parked beneath, the warmth in the air, the lightness of my movements when my body was clothed only in shorts and a shirt. How all sounds seemed far away, which made the silence there in the meadow seem conspicuous, almost penetrating. The sea opening up before us as we walked along carrying parasols and bags, how our gait changed as we stepped onto the beach and the sand gave way with each step, so that every movement forward also entailed a little backward thrust. And oh, the light blue sky, the wind that came fluttering in from the sea, the grey-white foaming waves that struck the beach, which together formed the rushing noise, at once near and far away, that had always sounded here, whether there were people to hear it or not, and which brought home, in a brief burst of joy, that we were on a planet somewhere in the universe.

We walked until we were far enough away from the other bathers, I jabbed the sharp end of the parasol deep into the sand, tossed a towel to each of the others, lay down in the sand and lit a cigarette while your siblings changed into swimming costumes and ran down to the water's edge. I didn't like swimming any more, anything below twenty-five degrees felt cold to me, and preferred to lie there on the warm sand just gazing at the sea, the sky, the bathers. Soon they would come running back, dripping with water, maybe shivering, and, screwing up their eyes against the sun, they would ask us either to come swimming with them or to buy them an ice cream.

'Do you think you could manage to get us some coffee too? One with milk and one without?' I said when a little later the girls stood in front of us.

'Of course we can manage,' the elder one said. 'But we don't want to. Why should you lie here doing nothing? We're not your servants, you know.'

'Do you want ice cream or don't you?'

'We want ice cream,' the younger said and looked pleadingly at her sister.

I regretted my ultimatum, for what might happen now was that she would sit down and say she didn't want an ice cream, even if she did. And then we would have created a situation out of nothing.

'Do as you like,' I said and took a hundred-kroner note out of my shorts pocket. 'Here, take this.'

They walked across the sand with their deep summer tan and spindly limbs, their long blonde hair tousled by the wind. Their brother came over when he realised something was happening, he asked if he could go too and started running after them.

'They're lovely, aren't they?' your mother said, she was sitting a few metres away, watching them go.

'Yes,' I said. 'They are.'

We sat there silently for a while. I had no idea what she was thinking about. I never did any more. I was no longer intensely preoccupied with her presence, which for so many years had always made me try to guess what she wanted, and to accommodate her wishes or to resist them.

The distance felt liberating.

But it wasn't constant.

'Did you want an ice cream too?' I said.

'No, I'm fine,' she said.

'You haven't started to regret it, have you?'

'Regret what?'

'That we're having another child?'

She gave me a long look, as if she was trying to figure out what I was thinking. Then she shook her head.

'There's nothing I want more,' she said.

I lay back so I could get the pack of cigarettes out of my pocket, lit one leaning on my elbow.

'Did you tell your mother yet?' I said after a while.

'Of course not,' she said.

'Well, shouldn't we?'

'Now?'

'Why not? She's your mother. And didn't we tell her just as early the other times?'

Her mother was an overwhelming positive force, and I thought that was what she needed to hear, how wonderful it was that we were expecting another child.

Having three children so close together had been like tying ourselves to the mast during a tempest. That we now, having come through the storm, were having another probably seemed thoughtless and overconfident seen from the outside, not least considering what had happened the previous summer. But your mother had never felt better than when we had small children.

'Maybe so,' she said and bent over her handbag, got out her phone, dialled the number and placed it against her ear.

I lay down on my back and gazed dully up at the sky, faintly sooty behind my dark sunglasses, while I listened to the conversation. She said that we were on Fårö now and everything was fine, the children were fine, and that she had something to tell her, some great news. I heard her mother's voice when she had been told, overflowing with joy and warmth. That didn't tell me anything about what she really thought about it, for she stood by her daughter no matter what, but judging from the timbre of her voice I got the sense that she was genuinely happy.

'What did she say?' I said when she had hung up.

'She was happy,' she said.

'That's good,' I said and sat up, pushing the burning cigarette butt deep down into the sand beside me. 'I'm looking forward to telling the children.'

'Yes, I wonder what they'll say?' she said and looked at me, smiling.

That smile felt good.

Just then the three familiar figures came into view further down the beach, they appeared over the sand dunes, and from the way the girls held their arms gingerly in front of them as they walked, I realised they had bought coffee for us after all.


Later that summer we were going to Brazil. By now you must probably be thinking that we went on holiday all the time in the years before you were born, but it wasn't like that. Usually we made one trip to Norway in the summer and stayed at home the rest of the time. But the previous year I had agreed to take part in a literature festival in Brazil and had asked to bring my family along, to which the organisers had agreed. They couldn't pay for the plane tickets, but they would cover hotel expenses, in addition to organising everything for us. It was winter in that part of the world, so after the festival we were going to fly north to where it was warm and spend a week at a hotel.

I had begun writing a kind of diary to you, or a long letter, about who we were and about what was happening here while we waited for you. I don't quite know why I did it, but I think the idea was that the other children would be pretty big when you arrived, ten, eight and six years old, and that they were already bonded together and had a shared history, and I didn't want you to become just an appendix to that, if you know what I mean. I knew that you wouldn't be able to read what I was writing about us until you were at least sixteen, so I guess it was mostly for my own sake that I did it, as a way of preparing myself, perhaps, a way of seeing what was happening here through your eyes. A way of clearing a space for you.

The initial phase of summer, when there is still a hint of chill in the air and the warmth vanishes as soon as the sun gets covered by a cloud or it begins to rain, so that it feels as if it is actually cold and that the warmth of the sun is just an unsuccessful measure that someone has put in place to remedy this – like one of those heaters for smokers that are placed outside pubs and cafés in the autumn and winter – didn't last long that year, the temperature began to rise towards the end of June, an area of high pressure settled over the country and stayed there into September. It was the finest summer since the one when your mother and I became a couple, ten years before, and intensely in love wandered around a Stockholm that was flooded with the light of the sun, which sank every evening into a fiery sea on the western horizon, and the nights that followed were warm and light and endless. But the atmosphere in Österlen was different, summer behaved differently there, created other moods, not like the ambience that arises between people in the spaces between buildings, with music streaming out of open windows, couples strolling in the otherwise deserted afternoon streets, parks overflowing with people, the smell of grilled hot dogs and smoke from burning charcoal, the sound of fishing boats knocking together down in the harbour, the hum of voices and laughter from the bars there, the pirate taxis cruising like sharks in the streets at night, the clusters of people outside the nightclubs and fast-food restaurants in the early morning, when the sky pales rapidly and the air fills with birdsong before you know it, and sunlight again cascades against every roof and facade and flashes against windows, antennas, the bonnets of cars and every stretch of water, and the big old leafy trees in the parks cast their dense and ample shadows across the otherwise blazing lawns. Summer brought some of this even to Österlen, for there too there were small towns and villages full of tourists, and there were small boat marinas with pubs and bars, but that wasn't the essential thing about it, that's not what gave it its particular aura – it was the vast blue sky, stretching out endlessly in every direction, and it was the fields beneath it, which also extended as far as the eye could see, full of dry golden grain which undulated like an ocean in the afternoon breeze coming off the land towards the farms that lay like islets of buildings and trees, separated from each other by several hundred metres. And it was the beaches that ran along the shore for kilometre after kilometre, in some places deep, like wide flat ribbons of sand beneath dunes piled up by the wind, in other places narrow, where the cliffs dived into the sea or where the forest grew all the way down to the edge of the sand. The sky was no taller, naturally, but here the sea was added to it, creating a world of space and light.

Imagine this landscape lying motionless, day after day. Not a breath of wind, just the still air beneath the dark blue sky, the saturated fields, the old trees in the farmyards, the narrow roads criss-crossing the landscape. And the chalk-white clouds sailing slowly by. The atmosphere it created, at least within me, was one of solitude and belonging at one and the same time. And of endlessness and closeness – everything was small, everything was local, houses stood singly, villages too, at the same time as the vastness of the sky seemed to drag everything towards infinity, not infinite space, but rather an infinity that had to do with time.

How can I explain that feeling to you?

Maybe you yourself will feel it one day, maybe not.

But the important thing to know is that it was good. When we woke in the morning, which always happened early, since your siblings, at least the younger two, woke up around six regardless of whether they had school or not, it was already warm enough for me to shuffle out to the mailbox and pick up the newspaper wearing only my shorts, and read it in the garden where the sun shone directly on the little space with chairs and table that we had made by the wall beneath the kitchen windows.

The bumblebees droned on their slow journey from petal to petal in the flower bed beside me, which ran all the way to the end of the house, where there was a little wooden stair-case leading to what had once, when there were three separate houses here, been the entrance to one of them. There, in the shade of the pear tree and the wooden trellis arch completely covered by a vine-like plant, your mother would sit drinking her coffee – unlike me she didn't like direct sunlight, her skin was pale and sensitive.

But since we had come home from Fårö, she hadn't sat there even once. Slowly darkness had fallen within her, and now it had almost engulfed her. It showed in her movements, which became slower and slower, and in the range of her movements, which became more and more limited, and in her speech, which almost ceased entirely. Slowly she descended the stairs in the morning, slowly she got the yoghurt out of the fridge and the muesli out of the cupboard, slowly she ate them at the dining room table while she stared straight ahead of her. The rest of the day she sat on the sofa watching movies. She ate lunch and dinner with us, and after dinner she went up to our room on the first floor and lay down. When I went to bed several hours later, and she lay there in the half-light with a frightened look in her eyes, she said in a low voice, I can't stand it. I said it was always like this, that it always passed, and that she just had to be patient. But I can't stand it, she said. What am I going to do?

There were hardly any points of contact between her life during those days and the life of the rest of the family. I drove into town with the children and bought a large and fairly deep swimming pool, inflated it and placed it on the flagstone path between the houses, filled it with water, which they at once, even though it was ice cold to begin with, started swimming in. I also bought badminton rackets and a net, which I set up in the middle of the lawn, where we played several times a day, either doubles or singles. Your siblings had friends visiting or visited friends every day, it was rare that there were fewer than four kids here at a time. We ate lunch and dinner outside, either in the little spot at the end of the summer house, which was set off from the rest of the garden by a gate and therefore felt almost like a separate world, or at the table I had placed beneath the apple tree at the other end of the garden.

The garden wasn't much to look at during the winter half

of the year, a fenced-in rectangular area that began between the houses and extended for maybe twenty metres, full of old, bent and leafless trees, pale yellow grass, and with the depressing sight of garden furniture covered with green mould which no one had bothered to carry indoors when at some point during the autumn it became too cold and blustery to use. But in the course of spring it underwent a total transformation, for it was so fertile here, nature's growth force was immense, so in summer the rectangular look disappeared completely, it was hard to see where the boundaries lay, green seemed to overflow everything, the trees and bushes formed labyrinthine paths, and everywhere there were flowers in clear, beautiful colours. The garden had been planned so that it was in bloom constantly from early March to late August, and in this way the colours seemed to migrate slowly, depending on which flowers were due to bloom, as if they sprang from a wheel, I thought at times, a roulette wheel turning extremely slowly. For a couple of weeks in spring the ground beneath the pear tree was completely covered with a carpet of blue flowers, which shone extra brightly because the lawn was still only grey-green and the leaves of the trees had not yet opened. Then came the crocuses and the wood anemones, followed by the tulips, and then it was May, and the rest of the garden exploded. The lilacs had their day, the roses theirs, and at the end of August, when one would think everything was over, the flower bed at the east end of the house, nearly covered by the branches above it, would suddenly begin to glow purple, pale red, pink and blue.

And when it rained! When the dense canopy of the trees was dark with moisture and the lawn was wet and heavy, and over this dark green glow there hung a grey sky, how marvellous these colours were then, so shimmering and fragile, almost as airy as the light itself.

But the garden was never more beautiful than in high summer, when the air stood warm and still between the trees, and the trees cast their deep shade into the green light, full of shimmering spots at the periphery, which quivered and shook in the afternoon when the offshore breeze began to blow. The children who ran shrieking in and out of the water from the sprinkler, or who slid around in the pool like little white seals, or who deep in concentration tried to hit the badminton shuttlecock that came sailing through the air, white and red against the dark blue sky. Or who lay each on their own blanket in the shade, on their belly with the computer in front of them and their legs bent at the knees, slowly and absently swinging them back and forth. The buzzing of the wasps, the bumblebees, the flies. The sudden, almost thundering noise when the two horses grazing on the other side of the hedge took it into their heads to gallop off, most often in the morning or into the afternoon, when it wasn't as warm, and the earth vibrated beneath the heavy pressure of their hooves.

The door always stood open during those days, the distinction between indoors and outdoors had been nearly erased, the children were barefoot or walked around in sandals, they wore swimming costumes, shorts or skirts, they ate sandwiches standing in the kitchen when they were hungry, or nagged until they were allowed to go to the shop and buy ice cream, which they ate with relish seated somewhere in the garden.

Between this external world and the inner reality that

your mother lived in, there was almost no connection any more. That's what happened, the connection was broken. What merely a few weeks ago had seemed beautiful to her, was no longer beautiful, it was nothing. What merely a few weeks ago had felt good to her, was no longer good, it was nothing. This was so because the beautiful and the good gain meaning through connection, through exchange, through what stands open between ourselves and the world. In themselves, objects and events don't mean anything. They become meaningful through the resonance they evoke. It is through resonance that we connect to the world, and that is what happened to your mother, the world no longer resonated within her. The connection was broken, she was shut out.

In the darkness she lived in then, only she and the pain she felt existed. I know this, my child, because I saw it. I saw that it was unbearable for her simply to be alive. She lay in bed all day long, and being there was unbearable, but she didn't have anywhere else to be, and the bed was associated with sleep, with darkness, which she longed for, since sleep was painless. But she could only sleep for so many hours a day, the rest of the time she lay motionless with her eyes closed up on the first floor, in the most distant room of the house, while the roof baked in the sun and made it as hot as a sauna, and all this time she must have heard the sounds from the world outside, which she no longer took part in. The kids screaming and shrieking and laughing as they played in the pool. The drone of the lawnmower as I pushed it around in ever-diminishing circles in the garden. The banging of cupboards being shut in the kitchen, the chinking of cups or glasses or whatever it was that was put back or taken out of them. The radio being switched on when I began to cook dinner, the voice of one of your siblings calling for help with something or other. The cawing of the colony of jackdaws, spreading like a parasol of sound over the houses in the evening, when they came flying from every direction and began settling down for the night. The distant rush of traffic on the road beyond, and once in a rare while the distinct drone of an engine rising above it, along with the sizzle of rolling tyres against the tarmac when a car drove down our street and passed right below our bedroom. The neighbours who had sat down in the garden each with a glass of wine and talked in voices that were certainly intended to be hushed but still carried a long way in the still summer air. The wasps that had nested in the air vent above the window, and buzzed back and forth all day long. The TV being switched on on the floor below. She must have lain there listening to all of this, for she lay in bed the whole day and the whole night. I don't know what all those sounds and all that life represented for her, what she thought about when she heard them. But if everything is black and everything hurts, and the blackness and the pain have grown until everything else is shut out, she probably heard nothing at all. And if she did hear, it must have been distantly, almost the way sounds from the real world can seep into dreams. And if she did identify a sound, for instance your siblings' shrieks of joy, it wouldn't have reached her as something good, something loaded with promise and love, but as something painful, that she herself wasn't a part of it, and never would be.

She felt like this once a month. Not always as strongly, but strong enough for it to mark her. In other words, I was used to it. And in a sense I had steeled myself against it, so as not to let the full extent of the pain in her eyes get to me, not let it mean to me what it meant to her. For what her eyes begged for was someone to love and care for her, and the loving care she sought was bottomless. There was also the practical side of life that had to be dealt with, not only did we have three children who needed attention, but we also had to earn money, in other words, to work. This gnawed at me constantly, and when darkness engulfed your mother, when the pain and the anxiety swept through her like an avalanche and she lay motionless on the sofa or the bed, I began to ignore it, in a kind of hope that some way or other she would realise that only she could drag herself out of it.

This time I was disappointed too. Life had been good for a long time, there had been a turnaround, and we were even expecting a child. What would become you already existed inside her belly. A new life. In the middle of a wonderful summer. With three delightful, suntanned children running around. In a magnificent garden. How could she turn away from all that? How was it possible that she didn't see it, how good everything was?

Mute and unmoving she lay in the warm, dim bedroom. Only rarely did she come down to eat. Then her face was expressionless, it looked like a mask, completely immobile. And her movements were slow, like those of a very old person. Slowly, slowly her hand lifted from the table, gripping the fork, on which a piece of potato was impaled, slowly, slowly through the air, towards her mouth, which opened slowly. If she looked at me, her gaze was filled with pain. If the children weren't there, she would sooner or later say in a low, almost inaudible voice:

'What am I going to do.'

'I can't stand it any more.'

'What am I going to do.'

'I can't stand it.'

It was like a prayer. It was as if she clung to those two sentences, as if they were all she had. To show her that I didn't accept it – the idea that that was all she had – I answered her in a loud voice. The loud voice was a rejection of her prayer, and of the premise of that prayer, that it was all she had. My voice was also irritated. I was fed up with all the whispering, all the immobility, the lack of initiative, the helplessness, the turning away.

'It will pass,' I said. 'It always does.'

Then I went to load the dishes into the dishwasher.

She came after me, taking slow steps, her forearms raised to a ninety-degree angle with her body, as if she was carrying something in front of her. But in her hands there was nothing.

I turned and gave her a demonstratively enquiring look.

'We can't go,' she whispered.

Her eyes were ablaze.

But not with light, they were blazing with darkness.

'What are you thinking of?' I said loudly and looked straight at her. 'Where can't we go?'

'The trip to Brazil,' she said almost inaudibly.

'What did you say?' I said.

'Brazil,' she said. 'We can't go.'

'Of course we can,' I said. 'It will pass. It's always like this. You lie up there in bed for a few days, maybe a week, and then it passes.'

'We can't,' she whispered.

'WE CAN'T CANCEL,' I shouted. 'DON'T YOU UNDERSTAND THAT?'

She looked at me. Though her eyes were full of suffering, I stared into them until she looked down. Then I turned away and continued loading the dishwasher. She stood behind me for a while, and it was unbearable, the impulse to turn round and give her what she wanted was almost impossible to resist. But I didn't turn, I poured the dregs of the water into the sink and placed the glasses upside down on the top rack. I opened the tap and held a plate obliquely against the jet of water, turning it slowly over the basin.

Behind me I heard her steps leave the room and go up the stairs.

I rinsed the rest of the plates, lined them up on the bottom shelf, dropped all the knives and forks with their handles down into the holder in the corner, poured detergent into the little hatch, closed the door of the dishwasher and set it going. Then I poured myself a cup of coffee and went out into the garden.

I sat at the table beneath the kitchen window for a long time, gazing into the garden. The sun stood in the sky to the south-west, and the shadows that stretched across the lawn were beginning to lengthen. The children were inside, but the traces they had left behind were many. A pair of sandals lying on the stone path in front of the blue plastic pool, with their pink straps and beige cork soles, one of them upside down. The white and orange Star Wars gun that rested against the trunk of the apple tree, the towels strewn in little piles in several places on the lawn, the bicycle I glimpsed behind the gate, lying on the ground with its spokes glittering in the sunlight. The stuffed animals they had taken out with them a couple of days ago and hadn't brought back in, down on the lawn in front of the brick wall at the other end, where they hardly ever went. A polar bear, a panda, a tiger and an owl, as far as I could make out. A sleeveless top, blue with white spots, also next to the swimming pool. A football in the bed of lavender, half a metre from where I was sitting, with a deep dent in the yellow leather, a blue basketball beneath the window of my office, the carrying case for the badminton rackets a little beyond that again.

The impulse to do good was still strong in me. The urge to go up to her and apologise, so that the balance was restored, required every ounce of willpower I had not to give in to it.

But if I did, it wouldn't be the balance between us that was restored, I told myself, it would be the balance within me. It wasn't in order to do good that I wanted to go up to her, it was because I was weak. I wasn't capable of being firm, I wasn't capable of being consistent, I wasn't able to resist. If she turned to me with that look in her eyes, so full of despair, so full of fear, I gave in and tried to give it what it wanted. And if I defied that look, which my reason told me I must, since what went on here was so destructive, a storm of guilt and shame broke out within me.

Why couldn't I just be good?

Why couldn't I just be kind and loving?

It did me good too, didn't it?

But it wasn't that simple. For if I gave in, I would allow fear to rule our family. This holiday trip had been planned for nearly a year. It was an experience I wanted to give the children, I wanted them to see South America, see Brazil, see Rio de Janeiro, a trip I hoped they would never forget.

Goddamned fucked-up shit.

I stubbed out the cigarette in the flower pot that stood on the ground beneath the table, sipped my coffee and lit a new cigarette, stretched out my legs. It smelled of new-mown grass, for I had mown half the lawn earlier that day. The lawnmower stood where I had left it, over by the furthest apple tree. Although my sense of ownership of what I bought as an adult wasn't as strong as that I had felt towards my things as a child, and I hardly thought of anything as mine any more, except clothes and books, I noticed that I enjoyed the sight of it standing there, metallic yellow amid all the organic green.

I stood up and walked across the garden, the grass soft and caressing beneath my bare feet, over to the lawnmower, which started up after only two yanks on the cord, since it had been used only a short while ago.

When the lawn was done, half an hour later, I let go of the handle so that the engine shut off, and pushed the mower across the short grass onto the stone path and over to the porch of the summer house, which was full of garden tools, buckets and basins, toys, suitcases and everything else that we didn't have room for in the house. I pushed the mower into this mess, closed the door and went into the living room, where the children lay sprawling in various positions on the big corner sofa, watching TV. I thought the sofa, grey and covered with stains, resembled a cliff, and that the children lay on it like lemurs. Their joints were completely flexible, and they were perfectly free in their choice of positions; your brother was lying on top of the backrest, with one hand dangling down along the side, one of your sisters was lying flat out on her belly with both hands under her chin, the other one was lying on her side with her head against the sofa corner and one leg resting against the top of the backrest.

'Everything OK?' I said.

'Yes,' your brother said.

'With you too?' I asked your sisters.

'Sure,' they said.

'Are you watching TV?'

'No, Dad, we're looking out the window,' your elder sister said. 'There's so much exciting stuff going on out there.'

'I guess I asked for that,' I said. 'I'm going to go out and work for a while. Come and get me if you need anything.'

'Where's Mum?'

'She's upstairs.'

'Why can't we go and get her?'

'Of course you can. It's your choice.'

I entered the little house which we somewhat euphemistically called 'the office' and wrote a few pages of my letter to you, about what we had done today. I didn't write one word about your mother or the state she was in. Then I went back into the main house, opened the dryer in the bathroom and took out the bundle of laundry. A little warmth was still left inside, and I pressed my face into the clothes, there was something childishly comforting about feeling the warm, clean-smelling laundry against my skin.

I tossed the bundle among the other clothes lying on the bed against the wall at the opposite end of the house from the living room, where your mother had her workspace. The room was L-shaped, and at the far end, beneath a window facing the garden, stood her desk, which we had bought at a nearby antique shop when we moved in, it was from the mid-nineteenth century and the piece of furniture we owned that I liked best. Age had made it rough and full of cracks, at the same time it was still robust and functional. The passing of time, I loved every trace of it.

The entire end wall was covered by a bookcase, on which she had placed pictures of the children, of me, in addition to her books, among which the proportion of women authors was considerably higher than on my shelves. Things usually changed a little in here when she was in high spirits, she became attached to other things then, bought other kinds of clothes and other kinds of objects, and I had realised that she had trouble reconciling herself to this when she came down again, probably also felt ashamed, since she would clear away the things and stop wearing the clothes.

These different sides of her were all part of her personality, but instead of being centred around a self, like modulations of it – I sensed, for instance, that some of the things she bought and brought out she liked because they reminded her of the good times in her childhood when she had been with her grandmother – they sometimes became a self in their own right and took her over completely.

She hated it. There was nothing she wanted more than to free herself of it. It ruined her life, she often said. There was something other inside her that took her over.

Who was she then, when she wasn't herself?

I began folding the clothes and laying them in little piles on the floor in front of me; one for the towels, one for bed-clothes, one for each of the children and for us. In the garden outside, the light from which came in through three windows, the colours had begun to grow dull. The grass must be starting to feel colder against the feet, I thought. While the air above it was still nice and warm.

When I went to bed that evening, not long after the children, your mother was asleep. I stood watching her for a few seconds, lying with one leg stretched out across the duvet, which she was somehow hugging close to her, and thought of you, that you were in there. Or the beginnings of the life that would become you. Three months was a kind of threshold, I knew; before that, anything could happen, and you, or the life that would become you, had only existed for six or seven weeks.

But I was sure it would be OK.

It was terribly hot in there. I leaned over and opened the window at the end of the bed, and an invisible corridor of something cooler appeared in the room as the evening air flowed in. Then I got undressed and lay down on my side of the bed.

She had opened her eyes and was looking at me.

'We can't go,' she said. 'Listen to me. We can't.'

'There are still five days left,' I said. 'Can't we wait a little and then decide when the time approaches?'

She closed her eyes for a while. When she opened them again, she said:

'I can't. I can't.'

I sighed and turned over on my side without saying goodnight.

Some days later we were in the car on our way to Ystad. She had an appointment with a psychiatrist, and I drove her. By then I had cancelled the trip to Brazil and told the children that there wasn't going to be any trip. Your younger sister cried when she was told, she had been looking forward to it so much. But it passed, and the summer was magnificent, hardly a day passed when we weren't on the beach, so there was no reason to feel sorry for them. The organisers sent several emails trying to persuade us to come anyway, first all of us, then just me. I had written that it was due to an illness in the family; to them that could have meant just about anything. But I was angry, at them, at your mother, at how the bad always got the better of the good.

This day too sunlight flooded the landscape. We drove through Sandskogen forest, where the crowns of the trees, dense with leaves, stood as closely packed as the walls of a tunnel. There was a lot of traffic, as always in the summer. We passed the camping site, which was crammed with tents and camper vans, and I glanced down the road on the other side, where the sea was visible as a glimpse of blue above the car park. But the sight didn't give me any pleasure, I was in a heavy mood, filled with a feeling of hopelessness, all the people in summer clothes standing in front of the kiosk or heading for the beach or sitting in the outdoor restaurant passed before my eyes without making any impression, I was completely indifferent to everything.

Your mother had been in therapy while she lived in Stockholm, and that was one of the disadvantages of moving to another town, that this relationship ended. She didn't start a new one in Malmö, nor in Ystad; the appointment she had now was at a walk-in clinic where she went to get her prescriptions renewed. She had asked me several times for help in finding a therapist or a treatment programme. I told her she had to manage it on her own. How could I set up something like that for her? I had no connections in that world. And why should I? She was an adult who was responsible for her own life, just as I was.

When she became really ill in Malmö, I called a psychologist, and he gave us an appointment, but it was pointless, the gap between him and her reality was too great. He wanted to talk about what it was like being married to a well known author, and how her lapses from the business of everyday life affected our relationship. She was beyond all that, mute and catatonic, at the edge of a sea of darkness that sucked her in, so who did what in the home was a matter beyond her reach.

That's how it was now too, as we sat in the same silence three years later, on our way to see another doctor. We parked in a large tarmacked square in an industrial-looking area, with warehouses and office buildings, and walked in the pointless blaze of the sun over to the building where the clinic was. The doctor, a young man with glasses who didn't look like he had turned thirty, sat behind his desk while your mother and I sat in separate chairs. He read the documentation he had about her while we sat there. They always did that, no one ever knew anything before we got there, and so they always asked the same questions. The doctor apologised, saying the staff turnover here was very high. He posed a few questions to your mother, who could hardly speak. He said he could see that she was deeply depressed, and therefore he had to ask her whether she was having thoughts of suicide. A long time passed before she shook her head. 'Can we trust you on this?' he said. 'That you're not going to do anything stupid?'

'Yes,' she said.

We drove to the pharmacy and got her prescriptions filled, then we went to get the children, they had been left with various friends, and your mother went back to bed.

Up until then I hadn't considered that there might be any risk of suicide. I had cast a surprised glance at the doctor when he put the question to her. I didn't think this was the case now either, not really. For the doctor it was routine, when someone was that depressed they were obliged to ask.

She had three children to whom she was everything, and another one in her belly.

I saw that she was struggling, that she could hardly bear it, but I also knew that she would manage, and that things would soon start to look up.

Still, I got out of the car before we left the next day, told the children to sit and wait a little, and went up to see her in the bedroom, where she was lying.

'We're going now,' I said.

She looked at me.

'You're OK with that, right?' I said.

She gave the faintest of nods.

'You're not going to . . . you know, do anything stupid?'

She shook her head.

'Well, have a nice day, then,' I said. 'See you in the evening.'

We were going to a water park that lay north of here, not far from Tomelilla. We used to go there once every summer. The children would start nagging us about it as soon as the season began. Not only did it have pools and slides of every description, there was also an affiliated amusement park, and the admission ticket allowed unlimited access to its various attractions.

Once when I drove past the entrance to it, I had misread the sign, I thought it said THE SUMMERLAND OF THE SOUL. It was mere wishful thinking, for what it actually said was THE SUMMERLAND OF SKÅNE. But the summerland of the soul! I couldn't imagine a more appealing name, I thought as we drove north with your elder sister in the seat next to me and the other two in the back. We took the route past Tosterup Castle, which had been built in the fourteenth century and lay two kilometres inland from where we lived, a yellow-brick building visible from far away, even though it wasn't particularly tall, with thick crooked walls, a tower and a moat, surrounded by a park, which seemed strangely out of place amid the farmlands. The castle was one of my favourite places in the area, both because it dated from the time of Dante, because Tycho Brahe had spent his childhood summers there, when Skåne was Danish and his uncle was lord of the castle, and because the social structure it attested to, a castle surrounded by forest and farmland, was so old and so concrete: it was there, to this small castle with crooked walls several metres thick, protected by a moat, that all local resources had flowed and from which all orders had issued. It was still privately owned, in fact a family was living there. The castle made me think of Montaigne's France, the torpid country life of that world, and of Calvino's short novels mixing history and fantasy, *The Baron in the Trees* and *The Cloven Viscount*, which I loved.

That something like this existed within walking distance of where we lived made me happy, although I hardly ever visited it except when we had guests. I saw it from a distance every day, driving to or from Ystad, a yellow wall in between the trees with a shimmering red roof that barely rose above the treetops, glowing in the sunset.

This morning we just sped past it, through the fields of corn that extended to the very edge of the forest, through a small settlement, across the train tracks and down to a little river or large brook where the vegetation was so sharply green that it almost seemed artificial after the cornfields' dry golden hues of dusty yellow and beige, overflowing with sunlight. Past some enormous, almost factory-like grain silos – or maybe they were actually factories? – onto a plateau, which in this flat landscape most of all reminded one of a high mountain plain, and out on the main road.

Your siblings were in high spirits, they talked and laughed, among other things about what they were going to do first when we got there, I heard them through the music, which was always playing while we drove.

We were going to meet another family there, your elder sister's best friend from the kindergarten she had gone to in Malmö, with whom she was still friends though they were now eleven years old, and her father and mother and little sister, they were spending a week at a cabin in Sandskogen just outside Ystad. Her father was the calmest and most balanced man I knew; he had studied philosophy and had written a thesis about Wittgenstein and Buddhism, which had also been published as a book, while now he was working on something very different, for a consultancy firm that he himself had started. Her mother, who was Danish, worked as a nurse at a shelter for addicts in Malmö. She was soft-spoken, a little shy, and together they formed one of those rare couples one meets where everything seems just right, where everything seems to be fine, one of those relationships one imagines will last their whole lives. Now there is more to people than what meets the eye, and nothing is easier than for a couple to put up a joint facade, I had known several perfect couples who were no longer couples, but there is one thing that is impossible to feign, and that is harmony and mutual trust.

I hope you will meet them yourself one day. They are not close friends of ours, I'm not good enough at talking to people to have close friends, and then there is also that I spend all my time on myself, which people notice, of course, so that no one takes that extra step. If someone does attempt to get closer, I usually withdraw into myself. That's how your father is, a little shy of people, not necessarily because I want to be that way, but because that's what I have become, and because that life, alone in front of the keyboard and the computer screen, is easier.

So then maybe I do want it after all? It's not a good quality, not something one wants to see in a person, but it will become a part of your life, and I think that is why I am writing this, as a sort of apology to you, when you read this one day. For when that day comes, I would like you to think well of me. And to think well of us, that summer when things were so hard for us.

I have grown more deterministic over the years, more and more often I think that one doesn't really have a choice, that who you are shapes your response to the situations that arise, and that you become who you are in response to the situations you have found yourself in and had to deal with in the course of your life. This is not a way of excusing wrong or bad or evil acts, but it is my experience that people are in a sense trapped within themselves, that we all view reality in particular ways and act accordingly, without the possibility of stepping outside ourselves and seeing that that reality is only one of many possible realities, and that we could just as well have acted differently, with as much justification.

That is why I wrote that self-deception is the most human thing of all. Self-deception isn't a lie, it's a survival mechanism. You too will deceive yourself, it's just a question of to what degree, and the only advice I can give you is to try to remember that others may see and experience the same things as you in an entirely different way, and that they have as much right to their viewpoint as you do.

But it is difficult. It may be the most difficult thing of all. Because it is just as important to be true to yourself, to hold on to your beliefs and think your own thoughts, not other people's. It is so easy to walk into one picture of reality and then let that picture sway you, even though on certain points it goes against what you really feel, experience and believe. What do you do then? The easiest thing is to adjust your feelings, experiences and thoughts, for a picture of reality is both simpler and more pleasant to relate to than reality itself. This brings us back to self-deception, the most human thing of all.

And perhaps the following is nothing but self-deception: the easy life is nothing to aspire to, the easy choice is never the worthiest solution, only the difficult life is a life worth living.

I don't know. But I think that's how it is.

What would seem to contradict this, is that I wish you and your siblings simple, easy, long and happy lives.

After driving for twenty minutes, the last few at a speed of a hundred kilometres per hour along the straight but hilly main road up the Fyle Valley, with the window open and air streaming into the car, we turned off to the left, drove down the long hill, turned onto a gravel road and entered a large open field that was jam-packed with cars. I found a vacant spot to park on the strip of grass by the fence, and that was perfect, for there the car was in the shade of a large tree, and it looked like it would be a burning hot day.

I opened the door and stepped down into the grass, opened the sliding door and let the kids out, grabbed the bag with towels and swimming gear, locked the car, lit a cigarette and began walking after your siblings, who were already far in front of me, heading towards the entrance, which lay on a hillock at the end of the field. There we were each given a bracelet before we went on, beneath the blazing sun, past an enormous playground structure with ropes and rope ladders and turrets and tunnels, where there wasn't a child to be seen; the rubber mattresses that one could jump down on must be scorching.

From there we looked down the hill, where the longest water slide ran in a construction far above our heads, it must have been a hundred and fifty metres long, you flung yourself down it on a kind of thin mattress and reached speeds that put it out of bounds to the children, thankfully, for otherwise I would have had to come with them, and the time was long since past when I enjoyed throwing myself off precipices, even under conditions as controlled and safe as here.

This water park was fairly old and worn, there was nothing high-tech, everything was manual and gravity-based, and that's why I liked it, there was something reminiscent of the 1970s about the whole place. And then there was lots of space, the slides and pools were spread out over a large area, with a little village of kiosks and cafés in the middle, and between the amusement park rides there were large park-like sections.

We found our friends on the lawn in front of one of the smaller pools, and I sat down with them for a few minutes while the children changed into swimsuits in the dressing rooms behind us. They asked me how your mother was doing, I replied that things were pretty good, but that she felt a little down just now. For some reason I felt a need to tell them that we were expecting another child, but of course I didn't, instead I talked a little about life in Malmö and about their younger daughter, who would soon be attending the same kindergarten as her sister, a parent cooperative, which meant that the parents' role was considerable – everyone had to take on a task, which in some cases demanded a lot of time, in addition to taking turns cleaning the place and being on duty there for one week every six months. I said I didn't miss that part, they smiled and said it wasn't what they were most looking forward to.

'But there were good things about it too,' I said. 'The children knew all the parents.'

'You're part of a parent co-op now too, aren't you?' he said.

'We've just left. He's starting school in August.'

'Oh, that's right. Time flies!'

'It does. Blink and they're gone.'

I looked down at their younger daughter, who was sitting in her mother's lap looking up at us, until she met my gaze, then she looked down.

'Well, you still have some time left with her,' I said, smiling.

Just then the girls came running over to us. They wanted us to join them, and I wrapped a towel around my waist, took off my shorts and put on my swimming trunks while I kept an eye on them as they ran over to the grassy hill alongside one of the other slides, which one sailed down on big yellow rubber rings, and felt my own reluctance. Not because it was scary, but because the water here was so damned cold.

We spent the morning by the pools and slides, had lunch and went over to the amusement park section, where we stayed the rest of the day. I drove a bumper car with your brother, while your sisters had one each, and I rode the roller coaster with them, and we sat together in one of those teacups that spin around really fast. I smiled at them when we started spinning, and they laughed, but suddenly it seemed as if a new gear had been engaged, we spun around much faster than I had expected, and for some reason I started to laugh, not controlled and measured the way I usually do, but uncontrollably, a huge delight bubbled up in me, and I laughed and laughed as we spun around in this garish teacup at this down-at-heel amusement park, while noticing that the children looked up at me in surprise for a moment, before they too began to laugh.

'You laughed so hard, Daddy,' your younger sister said when it was over and we got off.

'Yes, I did,' I said. 'It was fun!'

'You usually laugh like this,' she said, and did an imitation. 'Huh-huh-huh. But now you were laughing for real.'

'I guess I was,' I said. 'Did you think it was fun?'

She nodded gravely and looked up at me.

'Should we go one more time?'

When we drove homeward late in the afternoon, the children sat sleepily and silently in their seats. I hadn't thought about your mother for several hours; only as I got into the warm car, which was so familiar, did it hit me that she was all alone at home, in bed in the hot bedroom, filled with darkness and hopelessness.

I drove the thirty kilometres fast, through a landscape that also seemed drowsy and silent to me, saturated with sun, saturated with warmth, ready for the cool touch of the evening breeze, the starlit dark of night.

'Hello?' I called out as I entered the hall. 'We're home!'

There was no answer, and I went upstairs to the bedroom. She sat up halfway, supporting herself on her elbows.

'What time is it?' she said.

I saw at once that something had let go of her. There was more energy in her gaze, even if it was just as dark.

'A little past six,' I said. 'Did you eat anything?'

She nodded.

When I went downstairs, I saw that she had tidied the kitchen, done the dishes and put the crockery and cutlery back on the shelves.


The next day she got up in the morning, ate breakfast and went back to bed. I drove one of your sisters to her friend at Sandskogen, the other one went to visit a friend in the neighbourhood, while your brother was over at his best friend's place, so that the house was empty in the afternoon. Your mother came downstairs, she sat on the bench in the hall. It was as if all the energy in the house was being sucked towards her, into her dark eyes. She said she couldn't live like this any more. That it couldn't go on like this. I was standing on the floor, wearing shorts and a shirt, the door behind us was open, the air outside, filled with sunlight, was warm and still. She sat there in her pyjamas, looking down.

'I agree with you,' I said. 'So what are you going to do?'

'I don't know.'

There was a silence. After a while she said, 'You have to help me.'

'With what?'

'I need to get treatment. Sort out my medication. A therapist.'

'That sounds good,' I said. 'Have you thought of anything?'

She shook her head slowly. Then she looked up at me.

'You have to help me.'

'That may be part of the problem,' I said.

'What do you mean?'

'I can't really help you. This is something you have to get yourself out of on your own, you have to help yourself. I can support you, I can be there for you, but I can't help you. Only you can do that. You have to walk the last stretch alone. That's really what it's about.'

'What do you mean?'

'The illness has to do with you not taking responsibility for yourself. When you're down, you don't take responsibility for yourself, and when you're up, you don't take responsibility for yourself either.'

'But it just happens. Do you think I want it to? Do you think I want to live like this?'

'No. But I also don't think that you do enough. When it happens, you let go of everything. If you leave everything to the people around you, you'll never get better. You're the only one who can get yourself out of it. No one else can help you. You have to do it on your own. Because that's what it's about. I can be there, I can support you, but I can't walk the final stretch for you. Don't you understand that?'

She stood up and went upstairs to the bedroom.

I sighed and went out into the garden. I had spoken in a loud voice and offered her resistance, said exactly what she didn't want to hear. That she had to face it on her own. She wanted to hear that I felt sorry for her. She wanted to be cared for, she wanted compassion, help, she wanted to hear that it was something that came from outside herself to afflict her. As long as she met with only that kind of response, the illness would be nourished, it would go on and on, I thought. It was easier if it didn't have anything to do with her, for then she was merely to be pitied, then she could simply accept being looked after, as if by a parent. If it had something to do with her, she could confront it. Only then would she be able to get free of it.

That's what I was thinking.

I felt terrible, but I resisted the urge to smooth over what I had said, resisted the urge to look after her. I fetched the children, fried meatballs and cooked spaghetti for dinner, did the dishes, sat in the garden reading afterwards. When I went to bed, she was awake. I sat for a while reading newspapers on my Mac, she got up, walked past the sleeping children and went downstairs, where I heard her rummaging around for a while, getting ready for bed. I closed the laptop, placed it on the floor next to the bed, turned out the light and lay in the twilit room with my eyes closed as she returned and lay down next to me.

The children woke early, and I got up with them. There was dew on the grass outside, and the trees stood motionless in the light of the rising sun. I set out breakfast for them, of the very simplest kind, a box of cornflakes, a carton of milk, a deep bowl for each of them, a spoon. As for me, I drank a cup of coffee in the garden, where it was already warm in the sun, and where the insects were already about, buzzing around the flowers. My brother, your uncle, was coming today, together with his son, your cousin. They lived on the west coast of Norway, had spent the night in Oslo, and it was a long drive from there, so I wasn't expecting them until late in the afternoon. We had no plans for the day before that, but a trip to the beach or to the outdoor pool at Nybrostrand was probably unavoidable, I thought. Sometimes it was difficult to get your elder sister to come along; though there were few things she liked better than being in the water and there were never any fights between your siblings then, she didn't like to move, she didn't like change, and if she put up a show of resistance it might take a whole hour to get her into the car. But once we got there and were in the water, everything was fine. I always took care to tell her. Remember how good things are now! I would say. Remember how much you enjoy being here! OK, Dad, she would say. The next day the same thing might happen. But not always, sometimes everything ran smoothly and without friction.

On an ordinary day I would have worked in the morning, eaten lunch and gone swimming with the children after that, then barbecued in the evening. When your mother stayed in bed, I couldn't work, I couldn't let your siblings be entirely neglected. And now that we were having guests, barbecuing might be a little too much work, I thought, sitting there. Maybe shrimps would be better? With shrimps all you had to do was put them in a bowl on the table. And it was just as festive.

Shrimps, fresh baguettes, mayonnaise, white wine. And beer, as white wine wasn't really my thing.

We could stop at the fish shop at Kåseberga, they usually had fresh shrimps. Or the fish van at the market in Ystad. True, they didn't always have them, but Systembolaget, the government-owned liquor shop, was there too, so I would have to go there anyway. And then baguettes at Olof Victor's, the excellent bakery on the plain outside the village.

It would require some driving in the heat, but if the children had already been swimming, they would be in a good mood and put up with most things without protesting.

It felt good to know my brother was coming, I thought we could sit in the garden when the children had gone to bed, drink beer and talk.

The advantage of having siblings is that it is a lifelong attachment, and that nothing can break it. I hope you will have that experience with your own siblings. That was one of the reasons we had wanted more children, our thought was that you would always have each other.

While I sat there, the cat appeared on the roof, it peered down at me with its head poking out diagonally over the gutter. It was a Siberian forest cat, and like its Norwegian relative it could climb down trees head first. That's what it did now, for there was a little tree growing next to me, maybe two metres tall, with thin branches that swayed and trembled beneath the weight of the shaggy, long-haired animal. When it reached the ground, the cat slipped in through the open door, looking for something to eat in the kitchen.

I went in after it. It was standing on the low black wood-burning stove and miaowed when it saw me. I opened a new tin and could hardly get the food into the bowl, so eagerly did the cat push against my hand when it smelled the food.

The children were sitting in the living room, watching TV. They weren't really allowed to, but things had got a bit lax this summer. They had drawn the blinds, so it was dim as a grotto in there. I wondered for a moment whether I should switch it off, but I imagined the wave of protests that would rise if I did, and that they wouldn't find anything else to do, which would demand of me that I join them in some activity or other.

And I just didn't have the energy for that.

Besides, we would be out swimming almost the whole day.

That was enough sun, air and movement for them in one day, wasn't it?

But the blinds, damn it, I could at least raise the blinds! So they didn't seem so completely shut in.

I did, to protests which I ignored.

'One hour of TV is OK,' I said. 'Is that a deal?'

'All right,' they said, and I wondered whether they knew what I knew, that in an hour they would protest vehemently when I switched it off, no matter how much they agreed with me now.

I went into the bathroom, emptied the dryer, carried the clothes to the bed in the study, put the wet laundry from the washing machine into the dryer, turned it on, loaded the washing machine with what lay uppermost in the two wire laundry baskets beneath the window, sprinkled washing powder into it, selected a programme and switched it on.

When we bought the laundry baskets, I had wanted them to be plastic, I remembered. That was because the laundry basket we had had while I was growing up was plastic. Blue plastic mesh. I had thought of it as a little chap in the corner who willingly allowed his lid to be taken off so he could be stuffed full of wonderfully dirty laundry. So to me only plastic laundry baskets were the real thing. Can you imagine! I was over forty years old and completely ruled by a notion from my childhood. Your mother was able to persuade me that these were better, that the material was nicer and that plastic was really industrial-looking and ugly – she didn't say that, for if she had used the word ugly, I would have got all cranky – and now I could take pleasure in looking at these two baskets with their interlacing wire and beige cloth inner bags. But how many other notions were there, how many other odd preferences did I have that went back to my childhood, which I was ignorant of or didn't question?

I went into your mother's study and started folding the clothes on the bed, until I got tired of that and went back to the kitchen.

It was only seven thirty.

The morning hours were never a problem when I could write, then they simply vanished, lightly, as if I had hardly been touched by them. But in here I felt the full weight of time.

I took a few steps up the stairs so that I could see over the edge, into the bedroom at the end.

Your mother was lying completely motionless, sleeping.

I didn't want to wake her, I didn't want to tell her that she had to get up and help, that we were in this together. For if I didn't, just carried on alone, then I would be able to say, look at me, look at everything I'm doing, while you're doing nothing.

It gave me a good feeling. Anger in itself wasn't a good feeling, but anger mixed with triumph was.

If I sat watching TV with the children, the triumph was minor. If on the other hand I did something that demanded an effort and gave visible results, the triumph would feel greater.

What I really ought to do was tidy up the first floor. It looked terrible up there, toys and books lay strewn about everywhere, except for a path down the middle. But if I started tidying, she would wake up. And if she really wanted to sleep so badly, well, let her sleep.

Instead I began cleaning the kitchen. Even though we did the dishes every day and kept the counters tidy, gradually it still became overgrown, for piles of things from other parts of the house sprang up there, seemingly on their own, to say nothing of what went on in the cupboard where the rubbish bins stood, in the cutlery drawers, in the microwave, the oven and the fridge.

It was a big project, and it grew bigger, for if you cleaned one cupboard, it became obvious how dirty the others were. Although I was lightly clad, in my shorts, really a pair of cut-off jeans, and a wide, loose shirt, I soon felt hot, my brow gleamed with sweat, the shirt clung to my back. The better part of the irritation I had felt disappeared, for if I wasn't exactly relishing the work, there was still satisfaction in it, since for a long time I had been thinking that it had to be done, and now it was being done.

I took all the food out of the fridge, threw away whatever had expired, removed the shelves and washed them in the sink, cleaned the walls inside the fridge, replaced the shelves and put the food back in. Then I started on the cupboards and did the same thing there, threw out all the old spice packets, all the food items we didn't use and which had stood there for years, cleaned the shelves, put them back in. I wiped the cupboard doors clean, I took out plates and glasses and cups and cleaned the shelves.

Around nine thirty the children switched off the television by themselves and came out, said hi to me as they passed and continued out into the garden, where your sisters began to play badminton while your brother sat on the grass next to them and watched. After a while, as I was draining the grey water out of the sink and filling it with fresh, clean, warm water, they left the net and came running in, they wanted to know where their swimsuits were. I found them and handed them over, and they ran out again.

Shortly afterwards there was a knock on the door.

I hung the wet cloth over the edge of the bucket, straightened up, dried the sweat off my brow and went out into the hall.

It was one of the children's friends and her mother, they were standing in the doorway, dark against the blaze of sun behind them.

The girl was holding her mother's hand and looking over towards the pool, where your sisters were standing drying themselves off with their towels and staring back at us.

The mother asked if it was all right for her daughter to spend the day here.

I said yes, of course, that suits us fine.

'Mum, can I swim?' she said.

'Go ahead and swim,' I said.

She ran over to the others, and her mother took a step into the hall. She asked for your mother. I pointed upstairs.

'She's still asleep,' I said. 'And I'm cleaning the kitchen.'

'Well, say hello. Is it OK if I come and pick her up this afternoon?'

I nodded.

'Well, see you later, then! Just call if you need anything.'

She turned to go.

'Actually, there is one thing,' I said. 'We thought we'd go swimming. Can she come with us?'

'Of course,' she said. 'It's such a gorgeous day.'

'It is,' I said.

When she had gone, I continued to clean for a while, before going upstairs to wake your mother. It was nearly ten thirty, and the thought of just letting her sleep no longer felt good. That brief encounter in the hall had been enough for me to see myself from the outside, the neighbour's presence had somehow drawn me into the everyday world, where what I had been thinking didn't measure up.

I stopped beside the bed and said her name.

She didn't move.

I leaned down and nudged her gently.

'It's late,' I said. 'Maybe it's time to get up?'

She didn't react.

She used strong sleeping pills, sometimes it was almost impossible to wake her, and I thought she might have taken one more than she usually did, since she had slept so much lately.

I went back downstairs and was sitting on the bench in the hall when the children came running in and stopped in front of me.

'Can we have a bath in the bathtub?' they said. 'We're so cold!'

'You're *cold*?' I said. 'But it's so warm out?'

'But Dad. The *water* is cold.'

I supposed they were right, I had changed the water the day before, so I stood up, went into the bathroom and cleaned the bathtub, rinsed it, put in the plug and started to run a bath. The three girls got undressed and climbed in as soon as I had gone out. Through the window I could see your brother, he was dragging the hose with the sprinkler behind him through the garden.

I had to wake her up.

I went upstairs again, and now I was anxious, I thought something might be wrong.

I said her name again, louder, and I tugged at her shoulder again, harder. She barely turned her head.

I shook her again.

Nothing.

I became frightened. Could she have taken too many sleeping pills?

She was just sleeping heavily. There was no danger.

I went downstairs, sat down on the lawn.

Your brother was heading into the porch of the summer house, where the tap for the hose was located.

'What is it?' he said.

'Nothing,' I said. 'Are you going to water the garden?'

'Yup,' he said.

'Good,' I said.

I got up and went into the office, picked up the phone. Should I call an ambulance?

No, I couldn't do that. I couldn't bother them about something so minor.

She was just sleeping heavily.

At the same time I felt afraid, my hands were trembling more and more, and I could hardly stand.

I'll try one more time, I thought.

'Where's Mummy?' your brother said when he saw me coming. He was turning the tap on and off, so that the water in the sprinkler rose and fell.

'She's sleeping heavily,' I said.

Why did I say heavily? Why didn't I just say sleeping?

What shall I do.

Oh what shall I do, what shall I do.

I went up the stairs, through the messy room, and stood in front of our bed.

It was hot as an oven in there.

And she was lying just as still.

I bent forward, took hold of her shoulders and shook her hard.

She didn't react.

Just then your brother came up the stairs.

'What is it?' he said.

'Nothing,' I said. 'Mummy is just sleeping heavily.'

'Can't you wake her up?'

'No,' I said and walked towards him. 'But she takes sleeping pills, you know. And then you sleep really heavily. Come on, let's go downstairs.'

God, help me now, I thought.

Help me, God.

I need help now, God.

When your brother had gone back outside, and while the

girls were giggling in the bath, I got out the phone again. Surely they would understand that I was scared, even if it turned out that there was nothing to be afraid of.

I dialled 112. I got through at once. I said my name as I began walking across the garden so that your brother wouldn't hear what I was saying.

'It's about my wife. I can't wake her up. I think she may have taken too many sleeping pills. I don't really know what to do.'

'OK. Is she breathing?'

'Yes.'

'What address are you at now?'

I told them.

'We're sending an ambulance right away. It'll be there in ten minutes.'

Only then did I realise, my little girl.

Only then, when the ambulance was on its way.

I called the mother of your sister's friend and told her what had happened.

'Could you come and pick up the children? I don't want them to be here when the ambulance gets here.'

'We're coming right now,' she said.

I hung up and ran into the bathroom.

'Get dressed,' I said. 'Please do it as fast as you can.'

'Why?'

I told them that mummy was going to the hospital, that it wasn't anything serious, but that they were going over to their friend's house to play there.

They jumped up and began dressing. I went out and around the side of the house. The neighbours' car came careening at a wild speed, it must have been doing a hundred. They hit the brakes, the father got out and came running over to me.

'Where is she?' he said. 'I know first aid.'

'She's breathing,' I said. 'The ambulance will be here soon. You have to take the kids. Before it gets here.'

He followed me around the house. The children came out, and he hurried them along in front of him. They got in, and just as I could hear sirens down by the shop, they drove off.

It was like an inferno. Even though what actually happened was simple, a car came, filled up with kids, and left, and an ambulance arrived, it was like an inferno of movement. Everything else was erased as if by a white, blazing light.

Two men got out of the ambulance. They seemed calm. One of them asked me what had happened, while the other got out a case. I told them while we walked around the house. I showed them upstairs, through all the mess on the first floor and into the baking hot bedroom.

She was lying as before, as if nothing had happened.

I began to cry.

'It's like a sauna in here,' one of them said, shaking his head.

The other one began examining her.

'She's pregnant,' I said.

'Do you know what kind of medication she's taken?' the second one said.

'No,' I said.

'Where does she keep them? In the bathroom?'

'Yes.'

'Can you fetch them for us?'

I went downstairs to the bathroom and took the pill boxes out of the cupboard, they were open, there were some more lying on the corner of the sink. I put everything in a bag.

Upstairs in the bedroom they were calling her name loudly.

And she responded.

Her voice sounded muddled, but it was a response.

One of them came down the stairs, he was getting a stretcher. He said she would be OK. I gave him the bag with the medication.

I stood there listening to them working up there while the tears ran down my cheeks. Everything seemed to be sliding away in every direction, as if there was no centre, nothing to hold anything in place.

Then they came down the stairs with your mother strapped to the stretcher. She was still unconscious. Their heavy boots, the narrow staircase, how large the figure of your mother looked, like something in a dream where everything is out of proportion.

As we drove towards the hospital in the ambulance, what I could see outside didn't seem to have any connection to me. What had happened didn't either. They were just images, with no connection between them. I took a few deep breaths in an attempt to be present and take in what was happening. At the same time something in me wanted to remain on the outside, to push it all away or let it flow weightlessly through me.

The driver sitting next to me switched on the blue lights when we came out onto the main road. 'It's not really necessary,' he said, 'but there might be some traffic, so we may as well.'

We swerved around the cars in front of us in long gentle arcs. Most of them pulled over to the side of the road. The sea opened up in front of us and disappeared again as we drove in between the trees.

I had let her lie there.

She had taken too many pills, and I hadn't even noticed.

It was like a sauna where she had lain.

The sunlight dappled the foliage, glittered on the water, shone against the tarmac. We entered the residential areas outside the town centre. The people on the pavements peered at us as we drove past, just as I would have done if I was out there and not in here.

I had let her lie there.

It was like a sauna.

We drove up the hill towards the hospital, entered at the back, where a gate opened. We parked in the garage inside, and your mother was carried into a room where a team of doctors and nurses was waiting.

The ambulance personnel gave them a quick briefing, told them what had happened, what she had taken, that she was pregnant, before going out again.

I was standing by the wall with tears streaming down my face.

'Are you the husband?' one of the nurses said.

I nodded.

'You can sit there,' she said, nodding towards a chair in the corner.

'I didn't know she had done it,' I said in a voice that was barely audible. 'She lay there alone all morning.'

'It wasn't your fault,' she said. 'You mustn't think that.'

But that was exactly what I was thinking. I had let her lie

there for days, it was as hot as a sauna, and I hadn't even cared enough about her to notice that she had taken the pills.

But I didn't say anything, for what the nurse had said comforted me, even though it wasn't true.

Your mother was awake on the operating table but as if in a trance, she didn't understand the situation but accepted it, that there were doctors and nurses around her. After a while they left the room, and only one nurse remained. I had realised some time ago that her life was not in danger, then she would have been dead already. But how your life had fared, I didn't know.

Some hours later I climbed out of a car and walked into the garden at home. Your siblings were there, as well as their friend and her mother. Two of them were playing badminton in the sun, the other two were sitting in the shade watching. They were completely absorbed in the game, laughing and joking and focused on each other. I told the mother that my wife was OK and not in any danger. I looked down as I said it, for I felt a burning shame that I had exposed her daughter to this. When I looked up and met her gaze, I realised that she wasn't thinking about that. I almost began to cry again, but didn't, the children mustn't see it. She said they had been fine, they had played at their house for a while, then they had wanted to come up here. They had eaten, and they had been happy.

They stayed a little while longer, then she took her daughter with her and left. I told your siblings that their mother would be in hospital for a while, but that everything was fine and it wasn't anything serious. She had been in hospital before, so they weren't worried. Nor had they seen the ambulance or the stretcher, hadn't experienced any of the drama, so as long as I was calm, they were too. My brother and his son arrived later in the afternoon, and after we had exchanged a few words, standing in front of the door with the little pile of their suitcases and bags, where I told them a little more about what had happened than I had on the phone, they went out on the lawn and started playing badminton. I didn't understand how they could, for all I could see was the darkness in the light, I saw only shadows and the ghostliness of the deeply sunlit garden, but at the same time something in me knew that it was right, that for the sake of the children everything had to be as ordinary as possible.

I sat down in the chair beneath the kitchen window, lit a cigarette and watched them swatting the white shuttlecock with the red tip back and forth across the net, how each time it hung nearly weightlessly against the vast dark blue sky. The dark green shadows that fell across the garden. The sun that hung above the roof of the summer house, burning silently.

After we had eaten dinner outside, around a white table dappled with shadows from the leaves of the apple tree, which now and again trembled in the evening breeze, with the children squinting against the sunlight, I drove back to the hospital. I parked in the lot outside the entrance, and something about the warm tarmac, the dark blue of the sky, the long shadows and the fullness of the light from the low sun reminded me of summer evenings when I was growing up. When the day was really over, but it was so warm that we went for an evening swim in the sea, down by the bluff, the surface of the water dark closest to the rock, a luminous blue further out where the sunlight floated in broad bands.

The cool depths that lay there waiting.

I took the lift up into the building, walked down a corridor, opened the door of the ward and entered. A nurse who was heading down the hall turned to face me, and I asked for your mother.

She was lying alone in a room, it was white and filled with light from the setting sun. The duvet that covered her was white too, and the clothes she was wearing were white.

She was pale and worn out, lay with her head on the pillow, turned towards me as I entered.

'Oh, Karl Ove,' she said as I sat down next to her. Her voice was low, barely a whisper.

'Forgive me. You have to forgive me.'

She was crying.

I was crying too.

'I didn't know what I was doing,' she said.

'I know,' I said and took her hand. 'You mustn't think about it. It wasn't your fault. And you're fine now, everything went fine. Everything went fine. Everything went fine, do you hear me?'

THREE

Some days in spring it is as if the landscape here opens up in every direction, in the weeks before all the green unfolds in earnest, when the trees are still naked and the ground is still bare as if it were winter, while the sun shines with the fullness of summer and the light meets no obstacles, isn't bound up by the cornfields or the grass, the canopies of the trees or any of the other growing things which, as soon as they are here, create little pockets around themselves and become places in their own right. On such days in spring the landscape here seems placeless, and the volume of air beneath the sky, through which the light falls, is enormous.

That's how it was on that day in April as we drove along the road from the two little villages and with farms scattered on every side looking straight out at the sea, which was so dark that it didn't reflect the rays of the sun but lay there like a deep blue ribbon beneath the pale blue vault of the sky.

I stepped on the brakes as we approached the tricky crossroads, signalled right, leaned forward to see if any cars were coming, and turned into the coastal road, which ran along the artillery range all the way up to Kabusa, where it joined the main road to Ystad.

The air above the hills was faintly hazy, as it often is in spring and summer.

I turned down the music so I could hear whether you were awake, but although it was perfectly quiet in the back, it was impossible to tell, for sometimes you sat there without making a sound, just gazing ahead of you.

'Can you see the cows?' I said out loud.

There were maybe a hundred cows grazing here, a hardy, somewhat shaggy race, many of them light-coloured, some almost entirely white, most of them beige, nearly yellowish, a few were brown, but none tended towards red, like the cows I was used to from my childhood, these were darker, more earthy in colour.

I never saw them run, they stood there like statues, grazing or lying down to rest, in wind and rain, sleet or sun.

You didn't make a sound, and that was actually a good thing, I thought, for then you would be rested when we arrived to see your mother, who was looking forward to seeing you, and who might be a little disappointed if you were asleep then.

The car glided in between the trees, and the cows, the plain and the view of the sea all disappeared. The rest of the road to Ystad passed through Sandskogen forest, which Carl Linnaeus had taken the initiative to plant on his journey through Skåne in the 1700s, presumably to bind the soil and prevent it from being blown away inland across the fields.

Now it looked like it had always been here.

The branches of the trees were bare, and one could still see between them, unlike how it would be in just a few weeks, when the leaves would grow so densely that it would be like driving through a corridor. I shot quick glances into the forest, and due to the speed it was the space between the trees that emerged, and the forest floor, the beige carpet of long but flattened grass which the birches grew up out of. Something in me remembered the feeling of walking on that grass, from the time when as a boy I had walked around in the forest all year, when without realising it I was storing up experiences of nature, which could come rushing like an avalanche if something unexpected awakened them – the call of a bird in spring, the cool, almost glossy air on a summer morning, the smell of wet snow in winter, fog in the dark of an autumn evening.

I hoped that you and your siblings would also have this experience as adults. But that you would come to experience the time we had together now in the same way I had experienced my childhood, that was something I had difficulty grasping. Now, that was the everyday, it was prosaic dinners, driving here and there, evenings on the sofa in front of the television.

Would you extract magic from that?

Of course you would, for it didn't depend on the actual memories, but on the space they lit up in, the chords they struck, the resonance of another time. To my parents, the years when I was growing up must have seemed wholly unremarkable. The birdsong merely birdsong, the summer light in the mornings merely light, the fog on autumn evenings merely fog, the smell of snow just the smell of snow.

At the roundabout outside Ystad we turned off towards the town instead of taking the quicker route through the semi-industrial area to the motorway, for it cost us only a few minutes extra, and there was much more to see in the town centre. A long tree-lined avenue ran straight as an arrow towards the railway station and the port area, where the large ferries to Poland and Bornholm reared up above the docks, past the theatre which had been built around the turn of the previous century, when the theatre was still an important social institution, past the small boat marina and up the hills, where residential areas spread out on both sides and a new roundabout at the top connected the road from the town with the one from the industrial area and the road to Malmö and Trelleborg.

I liked this town, which had lain here peacefully by the Baltic Sea for hundreds of years, untouched by all the wars that had raged on the other side. Like all provincial towns it was inward-looking, and like all towns in agricultural areas it disliked new things; here everything was as it should be, everything bad came from the outside world. Everyone read the local paper, to them it was simply 'the paper', and how could anyone not like this daily enumeration of minor events, which are the same everywhere but which, owing to the force of the local, become meaningful in the place where one lives?

The most important reason I liked living here so much didn't dawn on me until several years after we had moved here. But it had to do with my childhood. I grew up ten kilometres outside a regional capital with around fifteen thousand inhabitants, in an area in the south of Norway that was full of tourists in the summer, nearly deserted in winter. The social structure here was identical, and that I hadn't recognised it at once had to do with the landscape being so different, making the structure hard to see. But Ystad was like Arendal, and now as then I liked to go into town on Saturday mornings, browse around a few shops, eat a bun in a pastry shop and overhear local conversations about local things, see neighbours meet and greet each other on the pedestrian mall, perhaps exchanging a few words and laughing a little before they continue their separate ways. One need only add the lifting of a hat, mutton-chop whiskers, a frock coat and galoshes if it's raining, and one is back in the nineteenth century.

When one grows up in a place like that, as you probably will, at first one doesn't see this, and when one does, in one's teens, it represents everything that is wrong with the world, everything one longs to get away from, because it is so indescribably small, so indescribably narrow, and when one is young, one is full of big emotions and longs to knock down all this pettiness and get away, out into the real world, where the things one is interested in, and everything one carries within oneself, all that is great and important, new and open, can be found.

At least that's how it was for me.

Then I grew older, then I had children, then I suddenly found myself in the same environment I grew up in, only seen from the other side. I didn't choose it consciously, I never thought, *I want to live the way I lived when I was growing up,* if I had thought that, I probably wouldn't have done it. No, it just happened that way. One day I was here. And if I hadn't liked how things were here, then one day I would have been somewhere else. So that must mean that I liked smallness, liked narrowness, that I liked sitting in the garden, far away from the important and principal places in the world.

In any case, what I was looking for was never the new, but the old truths as expressed by the new.

Not a sound came from you during the fifty kilometres of motorway to Malmö. I played music and looked at the landscape as I drove. The fields alternated between budding green and brown, in places almost black in the shadows near the edge of the forest, in other places so dry and light they looked almost like sand. In one place I saw two huge pipes the height of a man lying in the middle of a field, the sun shone on them so strongly that all colour had vanished, it was as if two pipes made of light lay out there, with the holes at their ends black as night. The forests that stretched inland resembled scrubland at a distance, they were leafless and faintly reddish in the light. Then came an area of dense spruce wood, the tops of the trees shone a pale green, while their bodies were filled with shadows. The sight awakened a kind of desire within me, just as cool dark water can if the surrounding landscape is full of light, for there is something about those brushstrokes of shadow, the feeling of depth when everything else is flat.

A dead rabbit lay by the roadside, a furry bundle with a light-coloured pool of blood flowing from it onto the grey tarmac. A few kilometres on, I saw a dead badger. It looked perfectly intact, as if it was lying there asleep in the sun with its black and white snout.

Outside Malmö, on top of a little hill where one has a view over the city and can recognise its three tallest buildings, the Turning Torso, the Crown Prince and the Hilton Hotel, which I always looked for, since we had lived right next to it for a few years, I turned onto the motorway to Helsingborg. Just as I accelerated in order to merge, a light on the dashboard started blinking. It was the low-fuel indicator, and I glanced at the gauge. The arrow had just entered the red zone. Strange, because usually I knew roughly how much was left in the tank, not consciously, but as one of the things one just knows, rather like the way one knows whether there is bread in the bread box or not, soap in the bathroom, milk in the fridge, how tall the grass on the lawn is, what day of the week it is, the time of night, roughly how heavy the bike you are about to lift into the boot will be.

I knew there would be a petrol station as we passed Barsebäck, and I was looking forward to it, then I could check on how you were doing, buy myself a coffee and maybe top up the windscreen washer fluid besides getting petrol.

Although the nuclear power plant wasn't visible from there, that's always what I thought about when I passed Barsebäck or stopped at the petrol station. I had only seen it from far away, from Malmö, and the sight always filled me with a vague unease. Not because I feared an accident, which would have disastrous consequences for the whole area, but because what they did in there was godlike.

As I parked next to the petrol pumps and switched off the engine, you began screaming in the back. I went round to the other side and opened the door, climbed in and bent over you.

'Hi there,' I said. 'Did I wake you so suddenly? We'll be fine, you'll see. Wait, let me get you some milk.'

I looked around for the bottle but couldn't see it.

Where could it be?

Oh no, damn.

I had left the bottle at the neighbour's.

I had a clear recollection now, that I had set the bottle on the table. And there was no memory of picking it up again.

'We'll have to buy a new bottle,' I said. 'There's a shopping centre not far from here. But first I have to get some fuel. OK?'

You continued to cry. I unbuckled your seat belt, lifted you up and took you out of the car, stood for a few seconds outside it and held you close. Luckily you stopped.

Holding you on one arm I opened the fuel cap with the other. Then I stood in front of the petrol pump and reached for the Visa card in my back pocket.

But it wasn't there.

That's where I always kept it, in my right back pocket, along with my licence.

Could I have put it in the other pocket?

No, it wasn't there either.

You were gazing aslant at the ground, and I held you up in front of me with both hands.

'There's been a small disaster,' I said. 'We don't have any money. And we're almost out of fuel. And we don't have a bottle for you either.'

You didn't meet my gaze, but continued staring diagonally at the ground.

'We'll sort it out, right?'

I held you close to my chest again, opened the door and put you in your seat. You started to scream. I strapped you in, closed the door, climbed into the driver's seat, started the engine and drove out onto the sun-flooded motorway again.

When I had paid the bill that morning, I had left the little card holder on the table and forgotten to put it back in my pocket.

I remembered the whole chain of events now but hadn't been mentally present at the time.

Goddamn it.

Damn, damn, damn.

I would have to get fuel soon, and you would soon need

milk. I knew no one in Helsingborg, and your mother didn't have any money, I knew that because she had asked me to bring her some the day before. I had planned to get some cash at the ATM at the hospital. Now I couldn't. Nor could I withdraw money at the bank, since I used my driving licence as identification.

Maybe I could borrow some money at the ward in the hospital? And then pay it back tomorrow. It wasn't like I could run away.

'Do you think you can hold on for another hour?' I said.

Your crying pierced my heart.

'We'll be fine, don't worry,' I said. 'It's just that your father is an idiot.'

I thought of putting on some music, but it seemed too brutal, drowning out your crying like that, so I sat there listening to it as we drove towards Landskrona, until maybe ten minutes later it gradually turned into a long drawn-out sobbing and then stopped completely.

You were asleep. And now what I wanted was not to wake you up, so when I put on some music again, I kept the volume way down, it was barely audible above the drone of the engine and the humming of the tyres rolling over the tarmac.

Just beyond Landskrona the road rises fairly steeply, and at the top, where there is a petrol station and some fast-food restaurants, is a view of Helsingborg. It is magnificent, at least I think so, for there aren't very many lookout points in Skåne, which is mainly completely flat, and the city's location, by the narrow sound between Sweden and Denmark, is unsurpassed. On the other side is Helsingör, with the castle where Hamlet lived clearly outlined, and between the two cities there are ferries running, big and white and beautiful against the blue water glittering in the sun.

Down the hill we drove, across the plain, up the next hill and off the motorway at the exit to Helsingborg, through a gently sloping, indefinable area, neither city nor non-city, until we came to the large roundabout, and the road seemed shut in by buildings for a few hundred metres, before opening up again near the port, glittering and shining in all that light, and we took off to the right and drove up the slope towards the hospital, which towered on top, colossal.

It was always difficult to find a place to park, since I no longer dared to drive into multi-storey car parks with our large car, after a couple of episodes when it was brand new when I had scratched it against a concrete pillar and a concrete wall.

Usually I drove slowly around the open car park in front of the entrance a few times, for sooner or later there was always a car backing out and leaving an empty spot, but on this day we were lucky, there were two empty spaces right next to each other, and I parked, switched off the engine and went round to the back to get you.

You were still asleep, and I unfastened the baby seat, pulled up the handle and lifted it out of the car with you inside, taking care to turn it with the backrest towards the sun, so that its rays didn't shine right in your eyes.

My movements as I walked across the parking lot with the baby seat dangling from my hand woke you up, but this time you didn't start to cry, you just lay there slowly blinking your eyes.

Thank goodness for that.

The nightmare scenario was that you would start scream-ing when we entered the ward, and that neither your mother nor I would be able to comfort you, since what you wanted was milk, and we didn't have any. Then the hospital staff would notice and draw their own conclusions. That we were unfit parents, that we weren't able to look after you, and they would know that there were three more children at home.

*Please, don't cry*, I thought as we entered through the automatic doors. *Don't cry. Don't cry.*

The entrance to the hospital was like a little square with a pharmacy and a café, and maybe around thirty people in it, some sitting around tables, others walking through the hall or standing in front of the pharmacy shelves or by the café counter. Some were sick, in wheelchairs or walking next to one of those rolling stands with bags dangling from them attached to their arms with plastic tubes, others healthy and fit, a couple of families with children.

'This is where you were born, you know,' I said, looking down at you. You lay perfectly still, staring straight ahead, then you waved one of your hands a little.

When you were born, we had spent a whole week here, and I had been here quite often before that too, visiting your mother, so the place was familiar. We entered the hall with the lifts, I pushed the button in the middle and kept an eye on the numbers above the different doors to see which eleva-tor was on its way down so we could get in front of it.

Neither the change of light inside the elevator nor the movements I made as we entered it made you aware of your-self and your situation, you merely gazed into the air and accepted whatever was happening. Maybe the feeling of hunger was just faint enough to be overshadowed by the new and continually changing surroundings.

Your mother saw us through the door as we came walking down the hall and at once went to fetch a nurse who unlocked the door and let us in.

'Oh my little heart,' she said, leaning over you. 'Oh how lovely you are. How lovely you are.'

I loosened the strap, lifted you up and handed you to her. She squeezed you tight.

'They've given us a room where we can be together, in there,' she said.

'She needs changing,' I said.

'I can do that,' she said.

'And I don't have any milk with me,' I said.

'You seem to be doing fine, though, don't you, little heart?' she said to you.

With the baby seat in one hand and the bag in the other, I followed you through the corridor, past the open TV room, where there were always people sitting, and into one of the rooms at the other end.

We stood admiring you as you lay naked on the bed, wiggling your legs. We talked about you and about the other children, and about the fact that your mother would be coming home soon, and the whole time you were lively and cheerful up until we were about to leave, then you began whimpering and seemed to be on the verge of crying for real. While your mother put on her coat, I went to speak to one of the nurses who was sitting inside the cage-like room, and who stood up and came out when I met her gaze.

I explained the situation, that I had forgotten my bank

card at home and that the fuel tank was nearly empty, the little that was left wasn't enough to get us home. Did they perhaps have some kind of cash box at the ward, from which I might borrow three hundred kroner so I could get home? I could pay them back tomorrow.

'I'm afraid that's not possible,' she said. 'We can't lend money to people who visit the ward, I'm sure you understand that.'

'But I'll pay it back tomorrow. I'm coming here tomorrow anyway. It's for fuel. I have our little daughter with me. It's kind of a crisis.'

'I'm sorry, I can't do that,' she said.

I looked at her. Then I turned and went back to the room. I hadn't said anything about not having any milk for you, then she probably would have called the Child Protection Service.

Your mother gave you a final kiss on the cheek, I strapped you into the baby seat, lifted it up, gave your mother a kiss and walked towards the exit, while you began to cry as you sat there, swinging back and forth.

Things would just get worse and worse, I thought as I waved goodbye and entered the lift. What the hell should I do?

'We'll be fine, you'll see,' I told you as we sank down through the floors and you lay there screaming, your eyelids puffy with tears.

Across the hall, out into the parking lot, over to the car, where I wondered for a moment whether I should lift you out and hold you close to me, then you might stop crying, but this would create false expectations, for sooner or later I would have to strap you in again and put you in the car, and then it would start all over again. Better to get it over with right away, I thought. I fastened your seat, started the engine and drove out of the hospital.

What should I do? Stop at the petrol station, explain the situation and ask them to let me fill the tank up on credit?

There was no way they would agree to that.

I turned into the road leading down to the city centre.

I could stop at a bank, after all there was money in my account, and there were photos of me on the Internet, I could ask them to check it.

It might work.

But where was Nordea?

I drove down the hill and turned right at the crossroads in the harbour, then drove along the wide road glancing up the side streets we were passing.

No bank in sight.

We followed the gentle slope up above the town, entered the streets just outside the centre, but the shops there were mainly car dealers and big supermarkets, not the kind of place you would find a bank.

You were screaming your head off in the back.

It was warm in the car too, maybe it would help if I rolled down the windows, I thought, and pressed the button in the door. At once the car filled with shuddering air, but there was something wild about it, something uncontrolled, and I shut the windows again, turned on the air conditioning instead, all the while steering the car back down towards the centre.

I parked at the bottom of the hill, close to a street I knew led to the centre, got out my mobile and googled Nordea Helsingborg, touched the map that came up and studied it for a while. The branch office appeared to be located a bit further down the road where we were standing.

'Let's keep our fingers crossed,' I said.

You weren't screaming quite as shrilly any more, perhaps because you were exhausted. I unfastened your seat, lifted it out, locked the door and started walking down the street with you dangling from my hand. Your face was wet with tears. You had never been without food for this long and must have been experiencing a feeling you had never had before.

I walked as fast as I could, your chair knocking against my thigh with every step. In order to vary my grip, sometimes I held it out from my body, sometimes close, sometimes in my right hand, sometimes in my left. The streets were full of people, without a care in the world they drifted past the shop windows in their sunglasses, carrying shopping bags, some holding ice cream cones. It was as if the two of us belonged to another world, I thought.

You began to cry again, but not furiously and with all your strength, as you had in the car.

Some people looked at us.

*Go to hell, you fucking idiots*, I thought.

If only the bank cashier would show some understanding.

This was Sweden, so my chances were slim, here everything had to go by the book.

So of course people went by the book.

Why didn't I? Why did I keep ending up in situations like this?

I walked faster. And maybe fifty metres further on, on the left, I saw the sign with the Nordea logo.

*

The place was full of people, exclusively old people, they sat on chairs by the wall or stood in front of the counter in the middle, filling out forms with slow movements. Many glanced at us as we entered, and I set the chair with you in it down on the floor as I took a queue number from the machine.

It would be a long wait.

I unstrapped you and lifted you up, held you close to my chest, walked around in there to give you something else to think about.

After maybe twenty minutes it was our turn. I went up to the counter with you on my arm.

'Hi,' I said.

'Hi,' said the cashier, a woman in her fifties.

'I have a problem,' I said.

'Yes?'

'I live in Österlen. And now I've run out of fuel here. And I've forgotten my card at home, and my ID. But I have an account with Nordea, and there's money in the account. Quite a lot, actually. Would it be possible to make a withdrawal without my ID? You can google me, if you want, there are photos of me on the Internet, so you can check that I'm the person I say I am.'

I blushed with humiliation.

She looked at me and smiled.

'That won't be necessary,' she said. 'Maybe you have a code? When you transfer money via the Internet?'

'I do,' I said. 'It's 4740.'

'Could you write down your name, address and account number for me?'

I did.

'How much would you like to withdraw?' she said.

I looked at her with moist eyes.

'I don't know. A thousand, maybe?'

'It's up to you.'

'Fifteen hundred, then.'

She typed for a while on her computer, printed out a receipt, counted out the money and laid it on the counter between us.

'Thank you so much!' I said. 'This is fantastic!'

She smiled and pushed the button which brought up a new number on the screen above us.

Half an hour later I was sitting next to you on the back seat of the car, pouring milk into the new bottle we had bought. I screwed on the top and stuck the rubber teat into your gaping mouth. You drank hungrily, with eyes that were open but not seeing anything in this world, and put your hands up around the bottle, even though you couldn't hold it on your own.

'Bloody hell,' I said and looked out the window just as two shadows were passing. Then I looked back at you.

'Is it good? It looks good.'

You suckled and smacked your lips and drank.

When the bottle was empty, I wiped your mouth and changed your nappy, and when I strapped you in, your eyelids had begun to flutter.

'What a day!' I said and got into the front seat, started the engine and drove out of town, up the hill and into the petrol station, where the numbers that seemed to run down the screen of the pump, and which usually made me slightly uncomfortable, since they represented money vanishing, now gave me a strong sense of satisfaction.

You slept all the way to Ystad and for the half-hour we stood parked beyond the railway station there. Maybe I should have let you stay in the car while I got out to fetch your grandmother, who was arriving by train from Stockholm to help us, but the thought that you might wake up and that someone might see you there, alone in the car, made me get out the chair with you in it and carry you across the road onto the platform, where only a few minutes later the train rolled in.

Your maternal grandmother had stayed with us regularly over the past year, since during that period your mother had alternated between being in hospital and being at home, and though I would have liked to manage everything by myself, I had realised that we needed help, for three children in a big house meant a great many practical chores in addition to my regular work, and when I was alone I just ran from one thing to the other without having either the time or the peace of mind to give the children the closeness and warmth which she, your grandmother, filled the house with when she was here.

She greeted you effusively as she got out of the train. I said nothing about our adventure, only that everything was fine and that your mother, her daughter, would soon be coming home, grabbed her suitcase in one hand, the chair with you in it with the other, and walked beside her over to the car.

When we came out of the forest and onto the plain where Österlen began, the sea in front of us was no longer dark blue, but sparkling yellow, almost white where the sunlight struck the surface. The blades of the wind turbines we could see far inland, above the tiny crowns of the trees, were turning rapidly in the wind.

*

The afternoon when I told your siblings they were going to have a baby sister, they were beside themselves with joy. It was more than they had dreamed of, having a little baby in the house. But your brother didn't believe it! I often kid with them, making up stories and theories which are so improbable they can't be true, or which, at least when they were younger, they never quite knew to be true or not. Your brother has never really liked this, maybe because there is something about it that feels unsafe, so his comment has always been, Dad, stop joking.

Now he refused to believe it.

I assured him that I would never kid them about something like that.

But no, this he didn't believe. Could he call Mum?

Of course.

I dialled the number, got through and handed him the phone. He took it, laid it against his ear and walked into the garden. I heard him mumbling. When he turned to us, his face was beaming with joy.

'We're going to have a baby sister!' he shouted.

'Tell us something we don't know,' his older sister said, laughing at his glee.

I thought to myself that I really should stop kidding him so much.

When you arrived, they had been waiting all autumn, and I think that made the months when your mother was in and out of hospital much easier for them.

It happened a month early, your mother was at home, and her waters broke at night, she woke me up and called an ambulance, which glided silently up the road outside the window, it was snowing and everything was soft and dark.

In the morning I told your siblings, they were excited, and while they were at school, where they probably told everyone they knew, I called your grandmother, who immediately got on the train. She arrived, and I went up to the hospital in Helsingborg. They had scheduled a Caesarean delivery for the next day, which was your sister's birthday. She would turn ten, it was a big day for her, and now I had to phone her and tell her that we wouldn't be there for it. That we would have to celebrate it a few days later. But then a midwife came on duty who couldn't understand this thing about a Caesarean, she induced labour, and you were born that evening. Early in the morning of the next day I drove home, stopped on the way and bought an iPhone, which for several years now we had promised to get your sister when she turned ten, celebrated her birthday and went back to the ward, where you lay in a little glass cage on wheels, wearing tiny pyjamas and a little cap, beneath a blanket, sleeping.

The enthusiasm your siblings showed then didn't die down; every single day, when they came home from school, they ran the final metres towards the house, threw their backpacks down, slipped off their shoes and hurried in to see you. You are growing up amid that enthusiasm, that joy. And it is unconditional, you haven't done anything to deserve it other than to exist.

This afternoon too, the first thing they did when they came home was to run in to see you. They were also happy that their grandmother was there. She got started in the kitchen right away, took food out of the fridge, put pots and pans on the stove, filled the entire house with her vigour. I carried you into the bathroom, put you on the changing table, carefully removed your clothes while you as usual lay gazing at the little revolving planes in the air above you.

Not once that day had I thought about the blood in the toilet bowl in the morning. Now I did, as if the memory was connected with the room, not with me.

I wasn't afraid any more, just annoyed that something wasn't working properly. That something always came up to upset things.

I leaned forward, pressed my lips against your warm belly and blew.

Your eyes widened with surprise.

I did it once more, and you laughed.

Then I put a nappy on you, a new pair of pants and a little sweater and lifted you up in front of the mirror.

'Who's that little cutie?' I said.

You weren't interested, and I brought you out into the kitchen, where your grandmother was chopping vegetables with the radio turned on and the window open.

'Is it OK if I leave her here for a while?' I said.

'Of course,' she said. 'You need some time to yourself.'

I brought the baby rocking chair from the living room, set it on the floor and strapped you into it. Then I boiled some water in the kettle, poured the steaming water over the reddish-brown instant coffee at the bottom of a cup and carried it out with me.

The garden looked different than it had in the morning when the sun had stood at the other end of the sky. The wind brushing through it now also made a difference.

I looked at the carpet of blue flowers growing beneath the still leafless pear tree and the plum tree beyond it. They shone in the light, their colour sharp against the green grass, but their shapes were soft. Daffodils stood here and there too, and tulips were coming up all over, still green and flowerless, but what a green! Moist, deep, a promise of life.

In a few hours, when twilight fell, the blue flowers would no longer shine, but glow faintly in the fading light, which also had hues of blue, and all this green would have vanished.

I walked along the stone path to the house on the other side of the garden. The air was sharp and cold in the shade, as so often in spring when the light and the air express opposite things. Summer, says the light, winter, says the air.

I closed the door behind me and sat down behind the desk.

It felt good.

I came in here whenever I could. When your mother was at home or one of your grandmothers was staying with us, I spent nearly all my time here. I took your siblings to school and picked them up again, but the rest of the day this is where I was.

I liked being alone, it was that simple, wasn't it?

My father, your grandfather, did too. In the house where I grew up there was a separate bedsit that was his, that's where he spent most of the time.

I didn't like that I was doing what he had done, I wanted to be a different father to you than he had been to us. But as soon as I shut the door behind me, it was as if you and your siblings disappeared, I didn't think about you any more, I entered my own world.

Well, not always. When things were at their most difficult for us, you were all I thought about. You who weren't yet born and your three siblings.

I remember standing here in the middle of the floor after taking them to school, I was completely torn up inside, and suddenly I began to cry. Not just the way I did when I was moved and my eyes grew moist, nor like that summer day when the ambulance came, when tears had trickled down my cheeks, but violently, with loud sobs, hard and contorted.

I can't take any more, I had thought then.

It was over in a few minutes. And it helped, the insurmountable once again seemed surmountable.

Neither you nor your siblings have ever seen me cry. I am the strong one, you feel, as children always feel about their parents, and it is, so I have thought, absolutely essential that you continue to feel this way, up until the point when as teenagers you begin to sense your own strength, when all my weaknesses will become apparent to you. Then you'll be strong enough to take it.

And then, if you have children of your own, it will begin all over again.

From the window above the desk I looked straight over at the kitchen, at your grandmother's shadowy figure moving slowly back and forth and cutting off the path of the light that entered the room through the window behind her. When they passed through the room, I could see the heads of the children too, and guess what they were doing from their speed and direction.

It felt as if we had come through something. But with feelings one never knows quite what they are about, why or how. The summer before, it was as if there was a fire inside me, as if everything that had become knotted together over the past few years had caught fire. When someone is going through a difficult time, the difficulties spread out in concentric circles and touch even peripheral situations and relationships. When darkness falls in one person, fire is lit in the other, and thereby all sense of normality vanishes, unless one struggles to stay within it, without necessarily even realising what one is doing. For on the one hand everything is as usual, and must remain as usual, on the other everything is an emergency. It is the friction between the two levels that starts the fire. It was like one of those fires that sometimes flare up in rubbish dumps and can go on for years. It might get smaller and smaller until it is just smouldering, but then something new happens, something dramatic, and it flares up again. No one could see it, no one knew about it, and no one could understand it, because everything looked the way it always did. But all relationships vanished in the fire. Friendship, family, neighbourliness. It took me several weeks to reply to emails from people I previously took care to stay in touch with, and if someone called, I didn't answer the phone. I attended only to the people who gave me something; those to whom I had to give something, I turned away from. It just seemed to happen, as is so often the case with actions that aren't good, they are kept out of sight of our consciousness. This partial blindness is one of the forms which self-deception takes. Of course it is also possible that I had never really cared about other people, only about myself, and that I now took the opportunity to live this out fully, that what happened was also an excuse to do away with everything except what I lived for, namely you and my writing. For there was something good about the fire too. I had never had as much reason to work, I have never had as much reason to live.

Now things seemed to be taking care of themselves, and the feeling that something was over, that something had let go, was strong on that spring day as I sat behind my desk and looked into the kitchen on the other side of the garden.

But I had thought that before, I realised, and then it had just continued.

I stood up and went back to the house. You had fallen asleep in your little rocking chair, your grandmother had covered your body with a blanket, and one of your hands lay on top of it.

'Little heart fell asleep,' she said.

'She's had a long day,' I said and went into the dining room to see if the table had been laid. It hadn't, so I got the plates out of the cupboard and started setting the table with them, scraped a few dry, flaky remains of food from one of them with the nail of my index finger while I looked out the window, the branches of the big chestnut tree were swinging up and down in the wind with the budding leaves like little pale green cocoons at their tips.

When the sun hung in the western sky, deeper in colour than it had been before that day, orange with a faint reddish hue, and the wind had died down completely, I dressed you in your little overalls while you lay in my lap with your head against my knee, put you in the pram and called your siblings.

Two of them came and started putting on jackets and shoes.

'Can you keep an eye on her?' I said and went to look for the third one. She was lying upstairs on her bed, playing a computer game. From the neighing sounds I gathered it had something to do with horses.

'Aren't you coming?' I said.

'I don't think so,' she said, looking up. 'Do I have to?'

'Well, you don't *have* to,' I said. 'But it'll be fun.'

'Ha ha. Your definition of fun is different from mine.'

'What is mine like, then?'

'Sitting in a log house in the mountains wearing a hand-knitted sweater.'

'Have I ever done that?'

'Maybe not directly. But that's what you dream of doing. Just admit it.'

'And you, what do you dream of?'

'My own room in a new house that doesn't have slanting walls and where everything is modern.'

'OK,' I said. 'But come over if you change your mind.'

She didn't reply, didn't even look up from the screen. I went down to the others, put on a jacket, my old trainers, and fished a brown cap out of the basket beneath the peg.

'Put your caps on too,' I said. 'It's going to get cold.'

'Did you bring money, Dad?' your sister said.

I nodded, put my cap on, opened the door with one hand and pushed the pram with you in it with the other.

Your siblings were already through the gate and heading through the garden at the back, where the shadows were long and there was already something hazy and faintly blurred about the air that hung motionless over the ground. We followed them slowly, you stared up into the sky while I stared at the gate that needed painting, and at the flagstone-covered area by the end wall of the summer house where in just a few weeks we would be able to sit and eat dinner, the weather-beaten teak furniture we had inherited from the previous owners, which was now covered with leaves, in places so dark and damp that they had almost turned to soil.

I ducked under the clothes line stretched from a tree to the fence of the neighbouring property, the only one of our fences that was completely white, for the simple reason that the neighbours had offered to paint our side too while they were at it, walked past the stone wall and out onto the lawn in front of the red-brick barn where the two horses sometimes were during the summer half of the year. From there I could look over towards the fire station, which was manned by volunteers, and where there were lots of people gathered outside, some with burning torches in their hands.

'Look at that, will you?' I said, bending over you. 'Are you doing OK?'

You looked straight up at me, smiling your funny smile.

I straightened up again and continued over to the fire station. Your sister and brother came towards us, they each wanted a torch but were afraid to take one themselves.

I did it for them. Nodded to those of the neighbours I knew, parked the pram a little distance away from them in a way that I hoped would seem casual, since I didn't know what to talk to them about but didn't want to seem aloof.

Your brother carefully stuck his torch down into the fire burning in a barrel, held it away from him in an exaggerated manner when it caught fire, walked stiffly over to the other children. Your sister did the same.

Several of the fathers of the children's classmates were dressed in full fireman's gear, helmet and all. Once I had been asked to join, but although there were few things more beautiful to me than fire and flames, I had turned down the offer. Sometimes I saw them sitting inside the station, sometimes outside with the two huge fire engines. I simply couldn't imagine myself there, being part of that fellowship; even if I had wanted to, it would have been impossible.

The thought made me smile. My idea of the fire within didn't come out of the encounter with real firemen very well.

A fire was something big. I was something small.

I leaned over the pram and stroked your cheek, I wanted another of those beaming smiles of yours. But I didn't get one, instead you twisted your head to the side and curled up your legs in one and the same movement.

In the middle of the road there was a handcart with a sound system on it. Next to it stood a man holding a large Swedish flag. Above the houses on the other side of the road the sun was descending, its rays no longer reached the soil but fell on the trees above us, which shone with a golden light against the greying ground.

A march blared out over the square, and the parade set off slowly into the main road and down the gentle slope, led by the man pulling the handcart and the man holding the flag. Torches, most of them held by children, burned here and there among the maybe thirty people walking downhill. Behind us there was a deep growl from the two fire engines, which were starting up and were to follow the parade slowly through the village.

It was Walpurgis night, the evening when spring is welcomed with song in Sweden. I hadn't known of the custom until I moved to this country twelve years ago, and it surprised me just as much every year. That Swedes of all people, who see themselves as the most modern people on earth and who want nothing to do with the past or with the archaic, for whom everything fixed and immobile is reactionary, even the body, which to them is not a tangible biological fact belonging to nature, but a cultural construction, a kind of artefact for which guidelines are drawn up in universities – that the Swedes, of all people, should gather once a year around huge bonfires, the most archaic thing of all, singing old songs in praise of spring, the very point being that even the new is also always old, this was hard for me to fathom.

But how glad I was that it was so!

As we paraded down the hill and onto the road that led out to the wide fields beyond the village, it was as if the old notions and the symbolism kept slipping in and out of the concrete reality they arose from. One moment I saw the flag, heard the march, saw the little parade of people, all of it gathered into one whole beneath the darkening sky in an agricultural landscape that opened up in every direction, while the sun hung like a reddish ball behind a veil of haze in the west, and then it felt as if something lifted inside me, a feeling that we were here, now, that this was our time. Then, in the next instant, I saw the idiotic handcart with its ugly sound system, the tracksuit bottoms, the all-weather jackets, the heads that seemed shrunken inside their caps, big noses, little eyes, fat cheeks, the old people trying to keep time to the music with stiff, faintly dragging steps, the smell of fertiliser, which was really the smell of shit, the hair of the woman in front of me, which a breath of wind flung across her face and which she couldn't quite get back into place, she tried once, but it blew back, and then again with an annoyed jerk of her hand, the father who shouted a reprimand to his daughter.

Then I looked around me, the fields at dusk, the big trees that grew along the brook and around the farms, the darkness rising everywhere and the red waves of light on the western sky. And I looked down at you, who still hadn't fallen asleep but lay on your back in the pram peering up at the little plastic figurine that dangled back and forth above you.

The first year we celebrated Walpurgis night here one of your sisters had given me her torch, which had almost burned down, and she was afraid to hold it with the flame so close to her hand. I took it for her. A few hundred metres further on, the road crossed a bridge over a little stream, and I thought I could toss the burning torch down into the water. When I stopped by the railing, my hand was stinging from the heat, and I flung the torch away. It didn't land in the water, as I had intended, but next to it, in the grass, which caught fire. I ran over the bridge, down the steep slope, kicked the torch into the water and trampled the burning grass while first the parade of people passed overhead, then the two colossal fire engines. Red in the face from the effort and from the looks I had attracted, I climbed back up again and scurried to catch up with the parade.

I thought of the episode as we walked across the bridge, as I did every year but never at other times. From there it was a five-minute walk to the bonfire we gathered around, in a field below a low ridge right by the stream. It was maybe three metres tall, broad and rounded like an old-fashioned haystack. The children tossed their torches into it, and it started to burn. People stood ranged along the gentle slope, maybe fifty all together. Above us the two fire engines were parked, and in the field a little beyond the bonfire a booth and a barbecue had been set up, the local sports club was selling hot dogs and soft drinks.

The sky above us was darkening fast, and the first stars had begun to appear in the east as the sun sank beneath the western horizon, veiled in red. The bonfire had caught properly now, it crackled and boomed and flung flames and smoke and whirling flakes of ash into the blue-black sky. The children ran around breathless and excited, shouting and screaming and laughing, for spring had arrived, filled with lightness, light and a billow of unaccustomed feelings.

You were still awake, and I stuck my head down to you, rubbing it against your belly, but you didn't laugh, just looked at me with big eyes as I straightened up.

'Dad, Dad, can we buy something?' your sister said, she was standing red-cheeked beside us, her white jacket shimmering faintly in the greyish light.

'Can you buy it yourself?'

'If you come with me.'

I followed her over to the booth, pushing the pram over the bumpy ground. It was cold beyond the heat of the bonfire. She got into line, and when it was her turn, I walked over to her and stood there while she ordered and paid, to give her the sense of security she wanted.

She shoved the hot dog into her mouth, grabbed the bottle and ran over to her friends from class. I remained where I was, standing with one hand in my pocket and the other around the handle of the pram. The triviality of the ketchup and mustard bottles, the blackened hot dogs, the camping table where the soft drinks were lined up, was almost inconceivable there beneath the stars, in the dancing light of the bonfire. It was as if I was standing in a banal world and gazing into a magical one, as if our lives played out in the borderland between two parallel realities.

We come from far away, from terrifying beauty, for a newborn child who opens its eyes for the first time is like a star, is like a sun, but we live our lives amid pettiness and stupidity, in the world of burned hot dogs and wobbly camping tables. The great and terrifying beauty does not abandon us, it is there all the time, in everything that is always the same, in the sun and the stars, in the bonfire and the darkness, in the blue carpet of flowers beneath the tree. It is of no use to us, it is too big for us, but we can look at it, and we can bow before it.

I stood there for a long time, looking at all the people standing about in the dusk, talking and laughing, the children scampering between them, the orange flames of the bonfire stretching into the darkness. When I bent down over you, tears were running down my cheeks. You smiled as you saw my face approaching, because you didn't know what tears were either.

# EPILOGUE

Today is Wednesday the thirteenth of April 2016, it is twelve minutes to eleven, and I have just finished writing this book for you. That is, I finished about an hour ago and went to school to pick up your brother, he felt nauseous and was lying on the couch outside the classroom when I arrived. Now he's lying on the sofa in the other house, watching TV. You're at the kindergarten. You are two years old, and what characterises you is that you are cheerful and energetic, from the moment you stand up in your cot in the morning and call for your mummy so she can come and lift you out, until you go to bed in the evening with the bottle of milk in your hands, without ever protesting. Some days ago you woke as I was getting up, it was a couple of minutes after four o'clock, I was coming over here to write. You stood up and peered out into the darkness beyond the window.

'Daddy, the moon!' you cried, pointing.

I stopped and leaned forward so I could see what you were seeing.

There it hung, the moon, shining in the dark.

I don't know why it made me happy, but it had to do with the way you were now orienting yourself in the world and could even identify the heavenly bodies. That it was personal, it was your moon. The beginning of speech is such a curious thing, that you suddenly say *dark* when we go out and it is dark outside, or *stars*, or, when you are sitting in the back of the car, which you still enjoy more than almost anything else, and shout LORRY! when you see a lorry, and in the next instant DADDY, THE LORRY IS STOPPING!

But it is your mother you spend most of your time with, she is the one you call for when something is going on, she is the one who comforts you and who gives you security. What happened that summer nearly three years ago, and its repercussions, are long since over. Your mother came home from hospital for the last time that following spring, since then she has been here, with you and with us. She has written two books during that time, one day you will read them. Your siblings play with you every day, you stand close to the wall with your eyes closed while they search for you, or they chase you through the rooms while you run as fast as you can, which isn't very fast for anyone else but you.

You can count to fifteen, but you always skip the number three. You know who owns every single thing in the house and like to name the owners, whether of shoes or jackets, toys or helmets. You have a stuffed animal that you drag around with you, a polar bear. You like to watch the Ice Age movies, and the first words you spoke, besides *Mummy*, were *thank you*. You like to twirl around until you get dizzy, and you like to wave to people, whether you know them or not. You like how you look in the blue dress, then you stroke your hands flat across your chest and say, *nice*.

Do you understand?

Sometimes it hurts to live, but there is always something to live for.

Could you try to remember that?

Also by Karl Ove Knausgaard